January 30, 2025

UNDER THE WING OF THE STORM

Also by J. E. Ribbey

The Last Patriots Series
American post-apocalyptic thrillers
Archangel
For You, My Dove
Rise of the Eagle
Operation Gray Owl

Young American Adventures
Middle grade historical fiction
The Innocent Rebel
Defiant Retreat
Under the Wing of the Storm
Deceptive Victory

Under the WING of the STORM

by J. E. RIBBEY

Soraya Jubilee PRESS

SORAYA JUBILEE PRESS
An imprint of The Jubilee Homestead LLC,
Stanchfield, Minnesota

Printed in the United States of America

LIBRARY OF CONGRESS CONTROL NUMBER: 2024906621

Print ISBN: 979-8-9899878-2-5
eBook ISBN: 979-8-9899878-3-2

Edited & cover design by Esther Ribbey

Cover image credit: General Herkimer at the Battle of Oriskany, original
painting by Frederick C. Yohn, reproduced by the Utica Public Library.

This is a work of fiction. Any similarity between the characters and
situations within its pages and places or persons, living or dead, is
unintentional and co-incidental.

To our own four young adventurers.

Chapter 1

April 29, 1777

It's been more than two years since Papa marched out onto the Lexington green. We haven't heard so much as a word on his condition, or whether he is even alive. Our world has changed so much since that fateful morning, but I suppose that is the way of life; nothing stays the same forever. All we can do is live as best we can in the midst of the circumstances we are given.

Today we received devastating news, the Continental supplies collected during the winter to support the spring campaign were destroyed by the redcoats in a surprise attack on the depot in Danbury, Connecticut. After a meager winter, such news has ravaged morale. General Benedict Arnold was dispatched as soon as General Washington had gotten word but arrived too late. In the end he was only able to pester the enemy as they retreated.

To make matters worse, we've been told General Wooster, who fought alongside Arnold, has been gravely wounded and is not expected to live out the week. The Continentals gave the enemy a fair bit of trouble, but it appears it was the Continentals who've come out the lesser for it. Although I despise the dreary cold of winter, I much prefer it over the devastation of war. It is regrettable that fighting season has come again so soon.

The camp has been astir since the attack on Danbury. Henry and Ben have been gone for two days scouting for provisions to make up for what we've lost. There is no doubt the redcoats will take advantage and come for Washington soon. The medical tent is bound to be filled to bursting in the coming months.

Abraham seems to have turned a new leaf since turning twelve over the winter. In the regular absence of Henry and Benjamin, he's determined to take his place as man of the family. As such, he's been most helpful to Abigail, quick to do his chores, and even keeps David in line.

The change in Abraham seems to have brought out a more subdued side of Mrs. Bell as well. In her words, he's "finally come to Jesus," and it has given her a new hope that all her labor has not been in vain. As for Adelaide and myself, we are as near to sisters as any two souls have ever been, something I had not expected to find in the midst of war. There are no secrets between us, as is only right in a true and meaningful friendship.

Theo has taken up residence at the medical tent, perhaps it is because he can keep a better eye on Lt. Davis; I still don't think he trusts him. Or perhaps it is jealousy of all the time I must spend there. Mama says it's more likely the food stores and medical supplies make the perfect habitat for mice and other vermin, and he finds the hunting easier. Whatever the reason, he *never fails to accompany Adelaide and I on our walks in the woods. He seems to delight in the sharing and keeping of secrets as well.*

As for myself, the long winter has me brimming with excitement for a new and adventurous year. I know that many trials await, but the Lord has already faithfully carried us through so many. Perhaps this will be the year we truly win our freedom.

Mercy Young, 14 years old

"Mercy, Mercy!" David shouted, bursting into the medical tent.

"What is it, Dave?!" Mercy asked, jumping up and spilling her lapful of bandages she was rolling up.

"Henry, and Benjamin just returned. They found some supplies, but they ran into a British foraging party and got into a scrape and Ben got shot!"

A pair of clopping horses came to a stop just outside the medical tent, and their riders dismounted as Mercy raced for the exit. The flap lifted and Henry and Ben stepped in, nearly knocking Mercy over, both of them looking bedraggled, but none the worse for wear, except for a small bandage on Benjamin's hand.

"See!" David said, pointing at the wound.

Mercy raised her hand to her chest to quiet her frenzied heart.

"It's hardly a scratch," Ben said, reaching to give her a hug.

"It's only a bit of rock spray," Henry added. "A musket ball struck the boulder we'd taken cover behind and a bit of it splintered off and hit him in the hand. We didn't even notice until the redcoats had scurried away, and we had a moment to catch our breath. It seems they're as desperate for supplies as we are."

Wrapping her arms around Ben, Mercy laid her head on his chest. "I can't have anything happen to you, Ben. You two have to be careful; I don't know what I'd do if you ended up like so many of these boys."

"I'll be more careful, Mercy. I promise," Ben said, letting her go.

"Did you shoot anyone, Ben?" David asked.

"I don't know, buddy; there was a lot of smoke."

"I feel it's better that we don't know; the conscience is a restless thing," Henry said. "You handled yourself well." Henry put his hand on Ben's shoulder.

"Well, I'm just glad you're alright," Mercy said. "Though you both could use a good bath."

"And some sleep," Ben added.

"Where's Abigail?" Henry asked.

"She and Mrs. Bell went for some necessities in Morristown. They shouldn't be much longer, just enough time for that bath. I'll have Abe bring up some water and get it warming over the fire," Mercy replied.

"A bath would be heavenly," Ben agreed.

When Abigail returned, it took all Mercy's strength to restrain 10–year–old David and keep him from running to her and spilling the beans about Benjamin's injury. The shock of such an announcement was sure to put her in a dither, better to let Henry deliver the news in his usual tactful way.

After Henry had had his moment, she released David to splash his way through the spring mudpuddles and deliver the news with his own particular flair. Even after Henry had softened the blow, Abigail still managed to fuss over Ben as though his hand would have to be amputated. Mercy just rolled her eyes; the boys never had it so good.

Then it was Adelaide's turn. She'd returned with Abigail and Mrs. Bell, and after Abigail was finished with Ben, she nearly melted with the thought that he'd been in danger. A smile crept across Mercy's face as she watched Ben take Adelaide by the shoulders, gaze longingly into her eyes, and promise her that he would always come back. Mercy would never admit it to Ben, but she was proud of the man he was becoming.

"Would you just look at those two," Abigail said as they carried the crates of supplies they'd picked up back to the medical tent. "Young love blossoming despite the mire."

"Who's in love?" asked David, splashing up to them.

"Oh, never you mind," Abigail chided. "You'll find out when it's time. Young boys seem to find no greater pleasure than to pester those who've entered into one of life's most precious journeys."

"Mrs. Abigail, I've never pestered a soul in my life . . . unless snakes and toads have souls, or bugs, and I guess there was that one time I pestered Mrs. Bell, but Abe says it's unlikely she has a soul on account she seems unable to experience joy."

"David Young!" Abigail blushed. "That is quite enough. Of course, Mrs. Bell has a soul, as she is one of God's precious children, and if you've pestered her, it would be only proper that you should go and apologize."

"I did apologize, like forty days, or even a month ago, and I haven't been a pest since."

"Well, I'm glad you had the good sense to make it right," Abigail said, setting down her crate.

"So?" David asked.

"So what, dear?" Abigail asked.

"Who's in love?"

Abigail looked over at Mercy, and then to David again.

"It's Mercy! Isn't it?!"

"What?! No!" Mercy said, throwing her apron at him.

"Then it's Ben!"

Abigail froze, glancing at Mercy again.

"Oh, ho ho! I knew there was something funny going on," he said, a grin of realization spreading across his face.

"David Young," Abigail said, taking a step towards him.

But it was too late; David ducked her hand as she reached for him and dashed out of the medical tent, surely to share the news with the world.

"Lord, have mercy," Abigail groaned.

"Looks like Ben had better have that chat with Mr. Bell as soon as he can," Mercy said.

Chapter 2

That evening, after they'd all returned to the wagon from their day's work, it was obvious David had made a critical logistical error in his rash excitement to share his news. He'd chosen his beloved teacher, Mrs. Bell, to be his first stop, and apparently, it would also be his last.

It turned out Mrs. Bell admired Ben as a young man and seeing that the war had given her the opportunity to observe many of them, she'd realized he may be one of the finest she'd yet had the pleasure to meet. As such, she'd made it clear that there would be no delivering of any news on the matter before Benjamin was properly granted permission to court Adelaide by her father. Mrs. Bell would not tolerate her daughter being the root of any camp gossip.

Thanks to Mercy's pet owl, Theo, their stew that night had a bit of squirrel meat in it, a luxury compared to what the rest of the army was eating. Mercy loved when the family was all home, sitting together around their campfire. It was all she needed; everything else in her life had become extra. Family meant everything.

Henry and Benjamin told stories of their forays into the countryside, their encounters with the redcoats, and the meager supplies their unit had been able to find. Abigail sat quietly mending a pair of Benjamin's breeches as she listened to their tales. Abe also listened intently, adding a bit of firewood every now and again as needed. Mercy knew he was patiently biding his time until he'd be allowed to join the army and tell stories of his own. War seemed a foolish test every young man was eager to take. Then sat David, still a little sore over the tongue lashing he'd received from Mrs. Bell, but unable to hide his curious excitement of their adventures.

"Mercy," Henry said. "Would you be interested in joining me on a supply run up to the tavern in Cambridge?"

"Henry!" Abigail chided.

"No danger this time," Henry assured. "Just checking on Mr. Hadley and the tavern, no spying, nothing out of the ordinary."

Abigail wasn't convinced. "Can't it wait? We'll *all* be going in hardly more than a week's time for the wedding."

"I may be called away in a week's time. No, this trip has waited long enough."

"Why does Mercy get to go?" David asked.

"You and Abraham already spent plenty of time at the tavern this winter. Mercy rarely ever misses a day of work, even on Sundays," Henry said.

"Will we be gone long?" Mercy asked.

"About four days, most of it in the wagon on the road."

Mercy hesitated, mulling over all the needs in camp.

"It might be my last chance before the spring campaign," Henry added.

"You should go, Mercy," Abigail encouraged. "It'll give you something else to write about other than the dreary weather we've been having."

"Alright," Mercy agreed. "I'll go."

"We'll leave at first light," Henry said.

In the morning Henry hitched up the team and they were off. Spring was a fascinating season, all the buds bursting into leaf and blossoms coming into bloom. Birds grappled with one another in the trees along the road. Little black and gold birds, red birds, blue birds, robins, and sparrows, all vying for a mate and the best nesting branches. Squirrels chased each other round and round on oak tree trunks, and spotted fawns danced alongside their mothers in the open fields.

The horses' hooves slopping and glopping in the mud of the road was oddly out of place amongst the chorus of springtime merriment. The team slipped and slopped their way up and down the hills, faithfully pulling the flatbed towards Cambridge. It was turning out to be a particularly wet spring.

Cresting a bluff, Mercy could see out over Long Island Sound. Merchant ships mingled with British frigates at anchor awaiting their orders for the spring campaign. Again, there was peace, enemies coexisting only a few short miles from one another, awaiting each other's first moves, and the commencement of war.

"Mr. Henry, do you think we'll win the war this year?" Mercy asked.

Henry shifted in his seat. "The king's army is unbeaten the world over, and our army has never won a war. It's David against Goliath, Mercy, but we can remain hopeful and confident, because that story has already been written. The difficulty of the task is not what should determine whether the task must be done or not, rather, it's the righteousness of the task which determines its worth." He put his arm around her.

"For the mass of men, most won't begin a task unless victory is assured them, and that leaves the majority of battles never fought. But a virtuous man will fight even the battles he must lose, because it is right that someone fight them. That is when providence takes the field, and battles which should not, are won. Our place in this conflict is not to fret about whether we will win or not, only that we fight because it is a just and good fight. When good men rise up and fight because it is just and right to do so, even boys can bring down giants," Henry said.

"So, are we going to win or not?" Mercy asked again.

"Ha," Henry laughed. "Mercy, I believe that so long as there are virtuous men who will take the field, we cannot lose. How long? That all depends on the king's resolve."

"Have you ever been to England?" Mercy asked.

"No."

"Has King George ever been to America?"

"Not that I'm aware of," Henry replied.

"What kind of king wants to rule a place they've never been?"

"He's not interested in the land, Mercy. He wants what he believes is his share of our economy. That's what the taxes are all about. The king believes he's intitled to a share of the profits of our labor whether we agree to it or not."

"Why would he think that?"

Henry sighed. "Because he's the ruler of Britain, and Britain has claimed the colonies in the name of the king, therefore making us all subjects of the king, and entitling him to a share of our profits, meaning whatever he and parliament deem right."

"So all taxes are bad?"

"Not all taxes. See, we're all part of a community, there are things we all share. Someone has to pay the soldiers in the army, the sailors in the navy, for roads, bridges, and other things we all share. A tax is a way for everyone who receives benefit from these things to participate in sharing the cost of building and maintaining them. The problem arises when the people are taxed unfairly, or for goods and services they do not receive a benefit from without their willing participation or consent. That is when taxation becomes theft."

"And we don't agree with the king's taxes?" Mercy asked.

"Correct, not that the taxes are wrong, but the king isn't willing to allow us to participate in the process of deciding what is being taxed and what it is being taxed for. He is taking the money out of our pockets whether we agree to it or not, and using his army to take it if we are unwilling to give it."

"So, the king is a thief?"

"As long as he chooses to behave like one," Henry replied.

"If he stopped, would the war stop?" Mercy asked.

"I believe it would, though it's hard to trust someone who's been a thief. I don't think the colonies would be satisfied with anything less than our sovereignty. The right to rule ourselves."

"And then we would be a good country?"

"Only so long as our rulers remain virtuous."

"It seems fragile," Mercy said.

"It is. Difficult to build, harder to defend. When the war is concluded, the real work will begin, without a common enemy, will we be able to remember the lessons we have learned, and keep from turning on one another?"

"I know I will never forget," Mercy replied.

Henry gave her a squeeze. "Nor will I, Mercy. Nor will I."

The team continued on in their monotonous way, mile after mile. Mercy snuggled close to Henry under the comforting weight of his arm. It was hard to believe it had only been two years since she and her brothers had set out from Lexington after their father was captured by redcoats. It must have been the Lord who'd led them to such a wonderful family in their hour of need. Henry was a deep well of wisdom, with the grace and patience to explain things in a way her innocent mind could understand them. She imagined God must be a Father in that similar way. Always patient and willing to teach a heart that was open to learn.

The sun rose high in the sky, its warmth only adding to the majesty of the moment. For the first time in three days, it wasn't raining. The rays drew out the smell of fresh earth, organic and alive, and it filled the air as farmers behind teams of oxen broke soft ground in preparation for planting. Mercy watched in awe as the curved metal blades effortlessly rolled the earth like waves in the harbor.

Robins and blackbirds hopped and swooped here and there behind a plough, pouncing on scores of worms unfortunate enough to have made their abode in the fields. In a small way she felt sorry for the little creatures, she could relate to having her world turned upside–down and being set upon by a swarm of red–breasted enemies. On the other hand, worms meant it was fishing season, and there weren't many things she loved more than fishing.

That night, Henry guided the wagon onto a flat spot of grass near the road and pulled the brake. After helping him unhitch the horses, Mercy prepared a frypan of bacon and potatoes, while Henry collected branches and got a fire going. After eating, they rolled out their bedrolls on the flatbed and laid down under the stars.

Chapter 3

The grays of dawn found Mercy and Henry harnessing up the horses and pulling back onto the muddy road towards the tavern. The air was cool and heavy with dew leaving everything damp even though it hadn't rained. Mercy hoped the sun would shine again and drive out the chill that seemed determined to burrow its way into her bones.

Here and there roosters crowed, and hens chased their chicks in farmyards as they passed. Cows grazed lazily on new spring shoots with their calves prancing nearby. Ducklings swam in little fuzzy clumps near their watchful parents, and lovesick frogs croaked. Everywhere, the world seemed to stir with excitement and life.

"Why are you turning here?" Mercy asked when they reached a fork in the road. "The tavern is that way."

"You're right," Henry said. "I'm surprised you remembered it. We're taking a small side trip."

"Why?"

"To keep a promise."

"What promise?" Mercy asked.

"You'll see." Henry grinned.

As they plodded along, Mercy realized she'd been down this road before, but she couldn't remember why. After a couple miles, a peculiar, sweet smell filled the air, and she inhaled deeply trying to place it. Then, as they rounded the bend, she saw it: row upon row of beautiful white blossoms.

"Mr. Gus's orchard!" Mercy gasped.

Trees, which had been gnarly and almost spooky two winters ago, now stood elegantly clothed in gowns of tiny white petals that blazed radiantly in the midmorning rays. The wagon rolled to a halt and Henry set the brake. Mercy staggered out of the wagon, not waiting for Henry's help, captivated by the beautiful sight. It was a beauty beyond words.

"Hey there, Henry," Gus called as he walked over to meet them.

"Hey there, Gus."

"What brings you folks my way on such a fine morning?" Gus asked.

"Just keeping a promise I made to Mercy, albeit a year late," Henry said. "How have you been, Gus?"

"Busy. The redcoats have bought out all my supply, I'm afraid I've got nothing left to sell the tavern," Gus said.

"That's alright," Henry said. "Times are tough right now, a man's got to do what a man's got to do."

"I heard you joined the Continentals," Gus said.

"That's right, figured I'd better do my part."

Gus looked over at Mercy. "Why don't you take a walk through the grove, young Miss. It's a magical world in there."

Mercy gave a polite curtsy and made for the gate. As she walked, she overheard Gus tell Henry that joining the Continentals was a fool's errand, and that there was a fortune to be made from the war if he had the good sense to pursue it.

Drawn by the beautiful flowers, Mercy passed through the gate and wandered down a walkway between two rows of apple trees. The first bees of the morning were already busily collecting pollen, and she stopped to watch one as it hovered from flower to flower. All of a sudden, satisfied it had filled its quota, the tiny little creature darted away from the tree back to wherever it had come from.

She wished Adelaide had come along, the two of them could have danced through the orchard together. She felt a little foolish dancing on her own; though, when she was sure no one was looking she allowed herself a little twirl. Gus was right, it did feel magical. If she were a princess, she would surely have an orchard as beautiful as this one.

It boggled her mind how many blossoms adorned each tree, hundreds upon hundreds of them. That meant that in the fall there would be thousands of apples. How did Gus ever keep up with so many? He could feed an army . . . perhaps he was. Is that what he'd meant when he'd told Henry there was a fortune to be made? But he was feeding the king's army?

She stepped back into the walkway and looked towards the wagon where Henry and Gus had been talking. Henry saw her and waved, and Mercy waved back.

"Everything is fine," she told herself, but she still felt uneasy.

Mercy doubted she'd ever forget her run–in with the Tories, and anybody could be a Tory. Since that time, they'd had complete battles against Tory militia. Not all of their enemies came from across the sea. The thought of Gus working for the British tarnished the moment some, though she tried to shake it.

Presently, a robin flew into the branches overhead, carrying a couple small twigs to add to its nest. A moment later a second robin joined the first, weaving its own twigs into the nest. She noticed several more nests in the trees surrounding her. The orchard was a robin inn, there were guests checking in all over the place. The thought made her smile . . . a robin inn, it sounded silly, and she decided she'd discuss the notion further in her diary.

At last Henry called out over the trees and it was time to go.

"Did you enjoy your walk, Miss?" asked Gus.

"Very much, sir," Mercy replied. "It was more beautiful than I had imagined."

"Well, I'm glad you got to see it then. These are ugly times, but there are still a few beautiful things to see if we know where to look," Gus said.

"Thanks again, Gus," Henry said, shaking his hand.

Henry helped Mercy back onto the buckboard and climbed in beside her. A flick of the reigns and they were off. The tavern wasn't far now, and Mercy looked forward to seeing Mr. Hadley again.

"Is Mr. Gus a Tory?" Mercy asked as soon as the orchard was out of sight. "I heard what he said to you about joining the Continentals."

"No, Mercy. He's just a man who's found a way to make a profit out of the troubles."

"But he's selling all his goods to feed the king's soldiers," Mercy replied.

"That's because the king can afford to pay full price for them. Gus is simply choosing to take the better deal."

"But that's the enemy!" Mercy exclaimed.

"Not his enemy," Henry replied.

"So, who's side is he on?"

"His own. He's choosing not to take sides. He'll sell to whoever is willing to pay the best price for his goods."

"But—but that's not right," Mercy protested.

"Why not?"

"Well, he wins no matter what. Without even having to fight."

"That's right," Henry replied. "Lots of folks are making that choice."

"But—isn't he your friend? How can he help the redcoats?"

"Mercy, he's just doing business. How could I call myself his friend if I didn't respect his right to choose how he lives his life? I'd be no different than the king."

"Don't you want him to help fight the redcoats?"

"Sure, we could use all the help we can get, but it's not my place to tell another man how to live out his convictions. Freedom doesn't mean everything goes our way, Mercy. In fact, many times it will not, but it also means that we don't have to live the way others would want us to either. That's what we're fighting for; for Gus's right to stay out of the troubles, and our right to fight. That each man would be responsible for his own life before God."

"If I had a friend in a fight, nothing in the world could stop me from fighting with them," Mercy said, folding her arms.

"I don't believe there's a soul who'd doubt that," Henry said, putting his arm around her. "Mr. Hadley sure wouldn't."

"I can't wait to see him again," Mercy said. "He and Mrs. White will be married soon. I used to think only young people fell in love."

"I think being in love keeps people young," Henry said.

"Yeah, Mr. Hadley acts like there's child trapped in that old body when he's around Mrs. White."

Reaching the tavern, Henry guided the wagon into the yard and pulled the brake. It was nearly lunch, and the tavern was already bustling with patrons. Henry helped Mercy down out of the wagon, and together they made their way to the kitchen door. When they entered, they found Mrs. White in a crisp apron, pulling a fresh loaf of bread from the oven. Mr. Hadley could be heard talking loudly with tavern goers at the bar.

"Bless my soul," Mrs. White said, setting down the loaf and giving Mercy a hug. "You must be growing by the minute."

"It's good to see you," Mercy said.

"You didn't bring that awful bird with you this time, did you?" Mrs. White winced.

"No," Mercy frowned. "He stayed back with Adelaide."

"I see . . ."

"Would you like some help?" Mercy asked.

"If you'd be willing," Mrs. White replied. "The fine spring weather seems to have everyone's spirits up. It's going to be a busy one today."

Mercy put on an apron and set to work peeling potatoes, while Henry entered the tavern to help Mr. Hadley. It felt good to be using her hands for something other than tending the wounded for a change. She enjoyed the familiarity of the tavern, it felt like home.

The hum and buzz of conversation centered around spring planting, the excessive rain, and the high prices of goods. The war had moved south, like a storm, and people here had weathered its coming and going and now it was little more than an inconvenience they'd have to bear.

As they worked, Mercy shared all the news from the camp with Mrs. White, concluding with their journey there and the beauty of the apple orchard.

"It'd be a right fine place for a wedding," Mercy said.

"It sounds divine indeed," Mrs. White agreed.

"I can't believe it's only a week away! Are you excited?" Mercy asked.

"I'm grateful," Mrs. White replied. "We spend so much time working together already it isn't that our relationship will change much I'm afraid. But to have a man who loves you and is as kind and gentle as Mr. Hadley . . . for that, any girl ought to be grateful."

"You are blessed to have him. He's one of the dearest souls I've ever met," Mercy agreed.

"I guess I have you to thank for that," Mrs. White said. "I've heard the story countless times of how you saved his life."

"Henry saved his life, I nearly got us both killed," Mercy corrected.

"That's not how Mr. Hadley tells it."

"Abigail says he's good a weaving yarns."

Chapter 4

*M*ay 10, 1777

This morning we woke at the tavern. Abigail, Mrs. Bell, Adelaide, the youngins and even Theo, attended Mr. Hadley and Mrs. White's wedding, or I guess it's Mrs. Hadley now. We ladies spent the morning helping prepare for the festivities, while Abe led the younger children on an adventure. Benjamin and Mr. Henry missed the wedding after all. They were called away with the other riflemen to South Carolina where bands of Cherokee Indians were raiding the homes of farmers and settlers at British behest.

The tavern was closed for the day and was transformed into a beautiful reception hall. The chapel, too, was adorned with freshly picked flowers. Mrs. White, as she was at the time, put on her best dress, and Mr. Hadley, his finest breeches and coat, the buckles on his shoes shining brightly. His gray hair was pulled back and held by a simple green bow. He looked as handsome and happy as ever I could remember.

The ceremony was a bit drab as Reverend Greene carried on in his usual monotone, that is, until Nathaniel's field mouse got loose. First thing it did was make a run for the safety of Mrs. McKinney's dress, and that's when things got interesting. Mrs. McKinney jumped straight up and fell backward over the pew, her legs kicking wildly in the air.

The poor creature then began running under the length of the pew, looking for shelter under every heeled shoe, you'd have thought it was a snake the way people were carrying on. The reverend himself got down from the pulpit and began chasing the critter with the gavel he kept to keep folks from sleeping during his sermons.

Abe and David dove under the pew, sending the ladies scattering from their seats. It took nearly a half dozen boys to chase the little critter out the door, where, unfortunately Theo, whose curiosity had been peaked by the commotion, ended its journey.

When the reverend returned to the pulpit, I saw Mr. Hadley praying silently as his face turned red as a beet from holding back his laughter. Even Mrs. White seemed to find some humor in the matter, but Reverend Greene proceeded with a sermon on the tenants of godly parenting. I thought Mrs. Bell was going to melt right onto the floor.

After the service, everyone made their way to the tavern to celebrate with the happy couple. Poor Nathaniel was marched up to the wedding table and forced to apologize in front of everyone. He hung his head and was near to tears, and I myself was moved to pity by his circumstances. Fortunately for him, Mr. Hadley has a soft heart and thanked Nathaniel for making his wedding one everyone would remember.

Mr. and Mrs. Hadley served their guests the finest the tavern had to offer, until everyone went home full and satisfied. If there were two humbler people on this earth, I've never met them. They deserve to be happy.

The ride back to the camp is sure to be an educational one, and I pray Mrs. Bell will take into account Nathaniel's youthful innocence, he meant no harm. As Mr. Hadley said, I doubt it is a wedding anyone will forget.

Mercy Young, 14 years old

It was midmorning as Mercy rushed through the remainder of her responsibilities. It had been two weeks since Mr. Hadley's wedding, and the post rider had arrived early that morning with a letter from Mr. Henry. It said the Continentals had beaten the Cherokee, and a treaty had been signed on May 20th with the tribe ceding their land in South Carolina to the Americans and ending the hostilities against the colonials. Henry and Benjamin would be coming home, and the post rider said they should arrive by evening.

Abe was taking David and Adelaide's younger siblings on a fishing expedition for Abigail so that Benjamin and Henry could have fresh fish for dinner, and Mercy hoped she and Adelaide could come along. As they finished their morning rounds, they saw Abe heading their way with several canes tucked under his arm, and a small flour sack that probably contained worms.

"As soon as Mable completes her chores, we'll be off," he called.

Mercy nodded, hanging up her apron. "We'll be ready."

When Mable finished, they started up the road towards the bridge which crossed the river at the north end of town. The weather had been dryer the last few days, leaving the road a gnarled mess of hardened wagon ruts. The river, which had threatened to wash out the bridge only days earlier, had returned to its regular depth and flow.

"I'm going to catch so many fish today," David said confidently.

"Not more than me," Nathaniel countered.

"You didn't even know how to fish before we showed you!" David retorted.

"And you didn't know before you were taught, Dave," Abe said.

David moved to make a rebuttal but thought better of it.

"Wow, don't you sound grown up," Adelaide said, raising her eyebrows at Abe, who instantly reddened.

When they reached the bridge, the fishing competition commenced. The younger boys immediately began racing up and down the bank looking for the best spots. Twelve–year–old Mable followed Abe to the other side of the bridge and together they fished an eddy created by debris left over from flooding, while Mercy and Adelaide fished near a piling.

The current of the modest river added an element of difficulty to their contest that was not lost on David and Nathaniel. Tempers flared as neither boy could keep his cork from floating away from their desired location. To make matters worse, Mable's cork began to bounce.

"That's it," Abe coached. "Let 'em take it just a little bit more. . . . Now!"

Mable snapped the end of her cane up into the air, while the fish on the other end made a run for the snags, nearly doubling it over.

"Hold on tight!" Abe said, moving to help.

"No," Mable grunted. "I want to catch my first one on my own."

"Okay," Abe said. "Lower your tip a little or it'll break your cane. It's happened to me bunches of times."

Mable obeyed as the fish tugged her cane back and forth, frantic to get itself free. Just then, Abe's cork plunged under the surface, and he had to dive to catch his cane before it was hauled out into the swirling water.

"Oh, it's another good one!" Abe cried, setting the hook.

In a few moments, they'd both battled their large trout onto the shore. Abe cut a narrow willow branch and slid the fish onto it, before rebaiting their hooks. Flipping their lines back out into the eddy, he sat back down next to Mable.

"That was a beauty of a first fish," Abe said.

Mable smiled at his compliment.

"Well, that's two," Mercy said.

No sooner had the words left her mouth than Abe's cork bounced again, and he set the hook.

"No fair," whined Dave. "Why do you get to catch all the fish?"

"Guess we picked the better spot," Abe answered, dragging his second fish ashore.

David collected his cane and dashed across the bridge to join them.

"There isn't enough room, Dave," argued Abe.

"There's plenty! You just don't want me catching any fish," David said, swinging his line around and whipping his cane forward.

"OHHH!" Abe hollered, jumping up from his seat, clutching his backside.

"What happened?!" Mercy cried.

"Dave just set his hook in my breeches," groaned Abe.

"He what?!" snorted Adelaide.

"Don't pull on it, Dave," Abe pleaded.

Mercy got up and raced across the bridge. Sure enough, David's hook was buried in Abe's backside.

"Let me see it," Mercy said.

"No," Abe backed away in embarrassment.

"Abe, Adelaide and I spend all day in the medical tent. There isn't any part of any man we haven't seen dozens of times. Now, we need to get that hook out of you before it gets infected, or you could end up in real trouble."

Abe looked around uncomfortably. "Could you send them all away first?" he pleaded.

"Alright, there'll be no gawking. All of you take yourselves over to Adelaide and try your luck fishing that side."

Reluctantly David and Mable made their way across the bridge. "I'm really sorry, Abe," David called.

"I'll be alright, it's just a little ol' hook," Abe assured him.

"Okay, Abe. I'm going to need your pocketknife," Mercy said.

"Why?" Abe whined.

"To cut the line . . ."

"Oh . . ." Abe blushed. "Here," he said, handing it to her.

Mercy flicked out the blade and with a brief sawing motion, she cut the line. "I'm afraid I'm going to have to cut your breeches as well, I'll mend them for you later."

Abe covered his face with his hands as Mercy gently cut the fabric around the hook revealing the area where it'd gotten lodged in his left cheek.

"This is humiliating," Abe complained.

"The point is almost coming back through the skin; because of the barb, I think it'd hurt less just to pull it through." Mercy winced.

Abe grabbed two fistfuls of his shirt, "Okay, Mercy."

"One, two . . ."

"Ouch!" Abe jumped. "Darn it, Mercy! I thought you were going on three!"

"And if I had, you'd have pulled away," Mercy replied. "It's through the skin now. All we have to do is pull it out."

Abe grit his teeth. "Okay, just do it."

As gently as she could, Mercy slid the hook through his skin and out. "There," she said. "It's all over."

Abe reached back his hand and messaged his sore buttocks. "Thank you, Mercy," he said, taking the hook from her hand.

"Untuck your shirt and it'll cover the hole until we get back," Mercy said.

Abe obeyed before tying the hook back onto David's cane. "We still need a few more fish," he said.

Abe invited David to take his place near the eddy, after assuring him that he was alright and there were no hard feelings. Nathaniel joined him, and in no time the fishing derby had resumed. Abe limped over to Mercy and gingerly sat down with her and Adelaide, content to let the younger boys fill their quota.

Theo danced expectantly on Mercy's shoulder as fish after fish was lifted from the eddy and added to the willow branch.

"I'm trying, Theo," Mercy apologized. "All the fish seem to be swimming in those sticks over there."

"Try taking your cork off," Abe suggested. "I brought a couple pieces of shot I could split and put on your line like we did when we fished in that harbor. It's the only way to keep our line from moving downstream in this current."

Mercy complied, and Abe split the shot with his pocketknife and pressed them onto her line. After adding a fresh worm, she swung it back out over the river and dropped it in behind a piling.

"It's much more difficult to discern a bite this way," Mercy said as the current tugged on her line, causing the tip of her cane to bounce.

It wasn't until the willow branch was nearly full of fish and they were about to start back to camp that Mercy's cane nearly jumped from the forked stick she'd used to hold it. Setting the hook, Mercy pulled a small silvery fish flopping from the water. Theo jumped from her shoulder, no longer content to wait, and dove onto the writhing fish.

"Theo!" Mercy shouted, lunging for the fish. But it was too late, Theo was all tangled in the line. "Argh!" she groaned.

"Just unhook it and let him have it," Abe said. "Then just cut him free, I can string the cane up again later," he said, handing Mercy his pocketknife for the second time that day.

Mercy did as Abe suggested, shaking her head at her feathered friend.

"I guess he just couldn't wait any longer," Adelaide giggled.

Chapter 5

When the six of them arrived back at camp carrying the day's bounty, Benjamin and Henry were already waiting with Abigail near the wagon.

"Isn't that a sight for sore eyes," Ben said, eyeing the stringer of fish. "My stomach's already growling."

"Benjamin!" David shouted, running to give him a hug.

Abe broke the willow branch and sent half the fish with Nathaniel to the Bells' camp.

"Why are you limping?" Abigail asked Abe, rising from her seat.

"Oh, it's nothing." Abe blushed.

"I set my hook in his backside," David confessed.

"Dave!" Abe hissed.

"Don't fret yourself, it wasn't your doing, Abe," Abigail said. "For once . . ."

Abe nodded.

"You'd better let me look at it all the same," Abigail said.

"Mercy already did."

"You could use some ointment," Mercy said. "An infection could be awful."

Reluctantly, Abe allowed Abigail to lead him over to the wagon to inspect his humiliation.

"So, tell me about your adventure," Henry said, setting David on his lap. "And then I'll tell you about ours."

After a dinner of fried fish in cornmeal breading, the Youngs sat around the fire hanging on Henry's every word as he detailed their battles with the Cherokee. The Cherokee sounded like brave and fearsome warriors. Henry said they ran about the woods, some of them half naked, screaming and whooping, appearing for a moment, only to disappear again. They fought with both primitive weapons and British muskets, not favoring one over the other.

The Cherokee didn't form up in lines like the British regulars, and the marksmen had difficulty confronting them. Many colonists paid dearly before they were able to bring them to terms. It seemed an awfully high price to give up so much of your homeland for a king who'd never grace your humble world. Henry said many of the Cherokee villages were raided and burned in retaliation, an eye for an eye that could only leave the world more blind.

Mercy shook her head as he concluded. There was so much suffering being endured by everyone. She could only imagine the fear and sorrow of so many Cherokee children who would soon be moving away from everything they'd ever known, never to return, and colonial children who'd had their parents murdered and homes burned. The consequences of a war they would never fight.

Abigail, too, seemed to feel for the families on all sides, while the boys seemed more interested in the romanticized notions of the battles themselves. Henry was reluctant to indulge them, and she felt that he too was grappling with the ugliness of it all.

The war wasn't always black and white. There were ripples, everyone was affected whether they participated or not; and the consequences, the consequences were shared by all the peoples. There would be no going back to the way things used to be, not for any of them.

When she went to bed that night, Mercy dreamed of Cherokee Indians mixed with the battle at Lexington. She'd seen Indians on numerous occasions, as they often traded with the colonists before the war. None of them had ever looked so fearsome as the warriors Henry described, with faces painted, and teeth bared. Now even the local tribes were forced to choose sides, pitting them against one another in the king's war.

Four days after Henry and Benjamin returned, orders came down from General Washington; the army would be moving out. Continental spies had confirmed that the British General Howe was preparing to move his army out of New York, where they had spent the winter in comfort and theatre, and begin his march towards Philadelphia, the Continental capital.

Washington knew Howe was a crafty general who controlled the battlefield by forcing the Continentals to choose between two objectives. This time he was forcing Washington to choose between saving Philadelphia or their supply line in Reading, PA. Washington, unsure of which location Howe intended to attack, decided to order the army to march to Middle Brook, NJ, the fork in the road south of New York, where Howe would make his choice. One road led to Philadelphia and the other, to Reading.

Mercy helped Lt. Davis load up the medical supplies, while Mrs. Bell and Abigail prepared their wagons to move out. Their portable city which had been home for so many months was reduced to a grid of muddy roads and grassless rectangles. The army was restless after the long winter, and everyone seemed to appreciate the opportunity to stretch their legs.

It would only take the army the better part of a day to cover the thirty miles to Middle Brook. Still, the move assured the Continentals that contact with the enemy was not a matter of if, but when. Nearly 8,300 soldiers marched in well–formed columns led by officers anxious to make their mark. Another two thousand followed in flatbed wagons, still suffering the ill effects of winter fever and smallpox, rendering them unable to fight.

From Middle Brook, Washington would have a better vantage point from where he could keep an eye on the nearly seventeen thousand redcoats and Hessians standing by in New York. Mercy found the numbers staggering, and the odds against them less than promising. Even at full strength, they were barely half the redcoats' number.

Another army of redcoats under the British commander and chief, General John Burgoyne, was marching south out of Canada towards Fort Ticonderoga, the fort which had once belonged to the British but had been captured in 1776 by Benedict Arnold and Nathaniel Greene who'd then sent the cannons to Boston to end the siege.

Arriving at Middle Brook midafternoon on May 28th, the Continentals set to work turning it into a defensible position. Mercy, Adelaide, Abigail, and Mrs. Bell helped Lt. Davis get the invalids settled and the medical things in order. Abe, David, and Nathaniel went to work gathering firewood for the cookfires, while the soldiers began construction of stockades, trenches, and artillery positions.

Mercy's arms and legs ached as they carried their last patient into the tent. With the warmer weather, many of them would begin to mend, so long as they could keep them dry.

Adelaide looked at her with a worn but resolute smile. "Home sweet home," she said.

"For now," Mercy agreed. "Hey, I've been meaning to ask you, did Ben manage to work up the courage to talk to your papa?"

Adelaide reddened. "He did . . ."

"And . . .?" Mercy asked, nudging her playfully.

Adelaide smiled shyly. "Papa said so long as we abide by Mama's rules, Ben has his blessing to court me."

"Awwwe," Mercy said, giving her a hug.

"Ben was still shaking when he gave me the news. Papa's a quiet man, but he's not a weak man," Adelaide snickered.

"What did your mama say?"

"Truth be told, she's fond of him," Adelaide answered. "Especially since she's had to put up with Abe for the past year. Ben's nearly a perfect gentleman, it's you and your owl Mama's afraid will ruin me."

"Well, like Abigail is always telling me, a girl's got to adapt during these troubled times," Mercy replied.

"And what are you two ladies snickering about?" Lt. Davis asked, approaching them.

"Nothing, sir," Mercy replied. "Just relieved to have all the patients back out of the elements."

"Ahh, yes," Lt. Davis agreed. "The weather has claimed enough of them already. If you've rested, I'd like us to make our rounds. There are sure to be those in need of care after such a ragged journey."

"Yes, sir," the girls replied.

Mercy enjoyed her work. The effort strengthened her muscles, and Lt. Davis was an apt teacher, sharpening her mind. The Lord had given her a caring, resolute spirit, and the battlefield proved her character. With her team by her side, she'd wade into the carnage left by the war and fight with all that was in her to put broken worlds back together.

They were warriors of a different stripe, battling infection, fever, and blood loss. Outnumbered, short on supplies, sleep, and sustenance, day after day, without complaint, the ladies rose to their task with smiles on their faces, and grace in their step. Ever present, ever willing, they were the angels of Washington's army.

"Hey, there, lass," a fevered man said as Mercy approached. "No need to waste time on me—" the man wheezed.

"You're not a waste, sir," Mercy said, gently dabbing his head with a cool rag. "If God has seen fit to put you on this earth, then I'm going to keep you here for as long as I can."

The man closed his eyes contentedly as she continued.

"I'll make you some tea, sir. It'll help with the fever." Mercy walked to the stove to fetch the kettle and work up a fever reducer when she overheard a colonel talking with Lt. Davis.

"We need every man you can spare," the colonel said. "We intercepted a courier carrying a message from parliament intended for General Burgoyne. They're growing impatient with his leadership, they want the rebellion squashed, or he will be removed from duty, and returned home in shame. They're coming, lad, and we can't afford to lose. I need men—these men, in the field."

"I assure you; we're working as fast as we can. The weather and poor conditions are more your foe than the redcoats. You must improve the conditions in the camp, sir. The boys must be kept dry. They must be fed and kept warm. They need good food and clothing. By the time they reach us, sir, the battle is already a desperate one," Lt. Davis said. "Our battle begins in the camp."

"There are no supplies, Lieutenant. We are not so privileged as to fight with what we want. We are bound by duty to fight with what we have. Now, get these soldiers up and out of bed, that's an order!"

The colonel turned and marched out of the tent, leaving Lt. Davis alone in his chamber. Mercy quickly poured the tea, but as she turned to walk back to the fevered man, Lt. Davis caught her arm.

"It isn't good manners for a young lady to eavesdrop," he said.

Mercy froze.

"And before you tell me you were just fetching tea, know that I know better."

Mercy nodded.

Lt. Davis relaxed his grip, sighing. "What does he expect us to do?" he asked. "This is medicine, not magic. The human body can only endure so much."

Mercy turned to face him. "He's just worried, sir. He has a problem that's bigger than him, and he's looking for someone to blame. I've done the same thing myself in like circumstances."

Lt. Davis looked back up at her admiringly. "I suppose he is."

"The nights are growing warmer, sir. These boys will pull through. That letter was not only a condemnation of General Burgoyne, it was high praise of our cause. We've already showed great determination beyond anything parliament could have fathomed, and we'll do it again. Just stay the course," Mercy said.

"Aye, Mercy. You're right, the warmer weather is just what we need. We must keep about our work, and let the Good Lord take care of the rest," Lt. Davis said.

"May I?" Mercy asked.

"Yes, go ahead," Lt. Davis said.

Mercy turned, walking back to her patient. Helping him sit up, she tilted the cup so he could sip the contents. She'd meant what she'd said, many of the patients would be back on their feet as soon as they could get their bodies strong enough. They just needed time.

She laid the man's head back on the pillow, saying a silent prayer before moving on to the next. With so many patients, it was all she could spare—a few moments of kindness—before moving on to the next.

Outside the medical tent, the work went on; horses clopped, wagons rolled, axes thudded, and shovels dug. Thousands of strong bodies working in unison towards their common goal. It was difficult to comprehend how different things were inside the tent. No one moved, no one was strong, nothing happened fast. Patience was the fastest road to recovery.

When she'd first began helping Abigail over a year ago, she'd missed being out of the action. But in time, she'd come to appreciate the importance of their work. The difference she made here would never win the war, would never be recorded in the history books, or inspire the next generation. But to the loved ones who prayed fervently for their husbands and fathers to return to them, her work meant everything, and it was to this end she served, hoping one day to have her own precious papa returned to her.

Chapter 6

June 14, 1777

Today a dispatch rider rode into camp and delivered a resolution to General Washington along with a beautiful new flag. The resolution read, "The flag of the thirteen United States shall be thirteen stripes, alternating red and white; that the union be thirteen stars, white in a blue field." The flag itself was more grand than any I've ever beheld. In the upper left corner, a rectangular rich blue field had centered in it a circle made up of thirteen brilliant white stars. From the top of the flag to the right, all the way to the bottom were bright red and white stripes boldly signifying our thirteen United States.

Henry said the flag was a clear message to King George that we no longer saw ourselves as subjects under his banner. That our people, while consisting of thirteen sovereign states, were also one. And those who would threaten the sovereignty of even the least of these states would have to face the wrath of the whole.

The spectacle seemed to inspire the soldiers as our flag no longer bore the British Union Jack. Surely General Howe's spies from New York will see it flying and report it; he'll soon know our rebellion is far from broken.

As I had suspected, many of our patients have recovered from the fever and pox thanks to the warmer weather giving their poor souls one less thing to fight. My wrists ache with the effort of writing so many letters home to loved ones from those returning to service. I wish the commanders would make better use of their time and teach their soldiers to read and write, perhaps then they would become something more than the lot of poor wretches they are.

Mrs. Bell, seeing the same plight, has opened an outdoor school for all the children in the camp. She may not be able to educate the current generation, but she's made it her aim to save the next. She seems much more contented now, seeing she's found her place. Many of her pupils are already reading and writing for their own parents who are unable to do so.

Apart from small foraging skirmishes the fighting has been light. Washington is ever on the move from hilltop to hilltop in reconnaissance of the enemy's movements. The army is ready to rip itself apart from anticipation and boredom as the enemy continues to delay any major action, and the Continentals lack the strength to engage. Henry says that with our few numbers our only strength lies in our defensive strategy.

All this means we are resigned to wait until the redcoats deem the conditions favorable. A notion I do not find settling. The Lord, knowing our every disadvantage, has kept us thus far. I pray He will guide our cause to victory.

Mercy Young, 14 years old

Mercy wiped her forehead with the back of her hand as she stirred the giant cauldron of rags and bandages. The weather had turned from warm to hot over the past few days and the job she'd been relieved to do during the long winter was now causing her to grow faint. Theo sat anxiously at the end of the crossbeam holding up the cauldron, watching the contents swirl in circles with anticipation.

"It's not stew, silly," Mercy chided. "Why don't you go make yourself useful and hunt us up a hare or something?"

Theo tilted his head sideways, staring at her blankly.

"Why don't you take him and the boys on one of your adventures," Abigail said, taking a seat beside her.

"Are you sure?" Mercy asked.

"These ol' legs could use a rest," Abigail said, taking the paddle. "It won't hurt me to do a spell of stirring while I'm at it."

"Thank you, Mama," Mercy said, giving her a hug.

"Stay away from the skunks," Abigail added.

"Yes, ma'am," Mercy replied. "Come on, Theo."

Theo jumped from his perch and glided to her shoulder. After collecting her brothers, they made their way towards the brook leading away from the camp. By now they'd discovered that much of the fun to be had in the wild took place where there was water, that and it was hard to get lost when you could just follow the stream back home.

Finding a suitable deer trail, they followed it to the northeast with nowhere in particular in mind. Abe had brought a length of twine with a cork and hook in case they happened upon a suitable pool. The shade of the tree canopy and gentle breeze seemed to rejuvenate her as they walked. The forest was brimming with the energy of life as all around them green plants contested one another for every available ray of the sun's light.

Hanging from Mercy's arm was a woven basket in which she placed the foraged young fern shoots, dandelion, green onion, and mushrooms; things Abigail and Mr. Hadley had taught her to forage. The forest was an abundant food store if a person knew where to look.

The boys played in the stream near her, flipping over rocks and chasing crayfish. It was one of the few things they seemed to never tire of. Mercy was just about to pull up a dandelion when she heard a commotion downstream. Theo heard it too, whipping his head around towards the noise.

Mercy held her finger to her lips to quiet the boys, pointing in the direction of the sound. There it was again, splashing, and . . . talking. Abe and David crept from the water and joined her on the shore. She knew they should go; there was no mistaking the clear, thick, British accents, but that adventuresome voice inside wanted to get a closer look.

"What do we do?" David asked.

"I think we should take a closer look," Abe said. "Might be a scouting party, they'd want details back at camp."

"I don't know," Mercy whispered, but she'd already received the confirmation she'd hoped for. "Okay, we'll take a look, but we have to be quick and quiet."

"Follow me," Abe said, creeping further down the deer trail.

"Abigail is going to lick us good . . ." David moaned.

Rounding the next bend, they crouched in the undergrowth. There, not thirty yards ahead, were three British soldiers stripped down to their breeches, having a swim in a deep pool. Their uniforms hung from the low branches of a nearby tree with their muskets and powder horns leaning against it.

"Looks like a foraging party," Abe said. "Look, they've got basket packs full of plants and things just like you have."

"Yeah," Mercy agreed.

"Okay, can we go now?" David whispered. "I don't want to get captured."

Mercy's eyes flew wide open. "Captured!" she whispered.

"Shhh," Abe said, glaring at her.

"Abe, we could capture them," Mercy said.

"Have you gone daft, Mercy?" he replied, but then he turned and looked back at the men playfully splashing one another.

"Ohhh, nooo," David whispered.

"You're right, Mercy. We could slip over there, fetch their muskets, and they'd be had," Abe said.

"What would Abigail say?" David pleaded.

"Let's do it," Mercy said, her heart already drumming in her chest.

"Dave, it's time to put all that practice we've been doin' to good use," Abe said.

"Follow me," Mercy said, picking her way through the underbrush towards the tree.

With every step she took, the voices in her mind battled it out. Ten more steps, nine, eight, seven. . . . The soldiers wrestled with one another only a few feet away, jockeying for which one was the best amongst them. Four, three, two, one . . .

Reaching the tree, she stretched out a hand and took one of the heavy muskets, carefully slipping it through the undergrowth to Abe, then she took another, and handed it to David, before taking the last for herself.

"Okay, now what?" Abe said in a trembling voice.

"When I count to three, we'll stand up and—and say halt," Mercy said as confidently as she could.

"Okay," Abe said.

David looked at them with fearful eyes, his musket trembling in his arms.

"One, two, three!"

The three of them stood from the undergrowth and shouted, "Halt!"

The men in the river froze their grappling and looked up at them wide eyed. For a moment, neither party moved, no one spoke, then one of the soldiers relaxed and started laughing.

"You gave us quite the start," he laughed. "But the king's muskets are not toys for colonial brats!"

A fire rose in Mercy's belly, and she cocked the hammer back on her musket, pointing it at the man.

"Are you a witch?" asked a second soldier, pointing in shock at Theo.

"A what?!" Mercy asked in disbelief.

"She's no witch," David countered. "She's my sister!"

"Is that right," the first soldier said. "And what are the three of you planning to do now?"

"You're coming back to camp with us," Abe said.

"Or what?!" the first soldier countered.

Abe cocked back his hammer.

The man's hands went into the air. "Easy now, lad. You don't want to be doing that. Just give us back our things and we'll go our separate ways, no hard feelings."

"You're coming with us," Abe repeated, swinging his musket from soldier to soldier.

"It's time you brats got what you have coming," the first soldier said, sloshing towards them.

Beside her, Dave cocked back his hammer and his musket went off, knocking him to the ground and sending a spray of water splashing up onto the soldiers where his musket ball hit the water. Mercy spun to look at Dave as the soldier froze in his tracks, throwing his hands back into the air.

"Alright!" the soldier exclaimed. "We'll go with you, there's no need for anyone to get shot."

Dave lay amongst the ferns rubbing his sore shoulder in dismay.

"Nice and easy," Abe said. "March that way, up the river, and keep your hands in the air."

The first soldier nodded to the others, and they formed up in a line staggering their way up stream.

"Dave, how about you collect their things," Mercy said. "I'll carry your musket."

Dave nodded, handing the weapon to Mercy. She slung it over her shoulder by the leather strap, keeping her own musket pointed at the redcoats, who were at the moment, no–coats. David threw their uniforms and pouches over his shoulder, collected their boots in his arms, and followed Mercy.

The walk back seemed longer than she'd remembered going, and it occurred to her that they'd probably started nearer the enemy camp than their own. Every now and again she looked back over her shoulder, the musket shot would have been heard by both camps, and as they approached their own, she could hear the drummer calling the camp to arms.

Up until this point, she'd been confident of their actions, but as the camp came into view, the knots in her stomach warned of the berating they were sure to receive. Still, if the war was to be won, and her father returned, then they'd just brought them three redcoats closer.

A sentry caught sight of them at the edge of camp and dispatched a squad of soldiers to intercept. The Continental soldiers marched towards them at the double–quick, surrounding their quarry with muskets at the ready.

"We'll take them from here, lad," a sergeant said.

Abe nodded, raising his musket, and the prisoners were marched away with heads hung. The Youngs followed the soldiers back inside the stockades where Henry and Abigail were waiting for them. Upon seeing them, David dropped his armload in the road and ran for Abigail, his face already wet with tears.

Mercy watched Abigail's shoulders relax as she wrapped him up in her arms, more relieved that they were alright, then angry they'd gone and done something foolish—again.

Henry walked over to Abe and Mercy, he looked them over for a moment before he took their muskets and slung them over his shoulder. "Collect their gear," he said. "And follow me."

Abe looked at Mercy mournfully before stooping over and collecting an armload of British uniforms. Mercy slung the powder horns over her shoulder and picked up their boots. Henry led them to a tent where the British soldiers had been sent for interrogation. Taking the uniforms from Abe, he stepped inside.

"I knew we were going to get it for this . . ." Abe muttered.

"It was as much your idea as it was mine," Mercy hissed. She looked at the ground. She'd done what she thought was right, but not what she'd known was safe. The truth was, she doubted she could have shot one of the soldiers, and if it wasn't for David's accidental discharge, they may have ended up in a bad way. She shouldn't have been so foolish as to believe the redcoats would have respected a bunch of kids.

"Still," Abe said. "We did just capture three British soldiers." A wily smile spread across his face.

Mercy smiled back.

In a moment, Henry returned from the tent, his expression refusing to betray his thoughts. "Follow me," he said again.

He led them to the far edge of the training field, away from the prying eyes and ears of those in camp, with nothing better to do than watch the spectacle and spread gossip. At last, he stopped, and turned to face them. His expression was stern, but fair.

"I'm sorr—" Abe began, but Henry held up his hand to stop him.

Chapter 7

D o you know why I brought you all this way?" Henry asked, eyeing each of them.

Mercy dropped her head, looking at her toes.

"So no one would hear what you have to say, sir?" Abe asked.

"I brought you here so that I wouldn't shame you," he said. "And, because my temper at the first, was not in any condition to respond to your behavior. And I did not want to proceed in a manner that I would only regret as I lay on my pillow."

Abe nodded, but Mercy could not make herself face him. She could hear the emotion in his voice, and the care he'd taken to answer the situation correctly. She'd grieved him, and somehow that was more than enough to overshadow the success of their foray.

"I don't want to assume upon you evils you have not committed," Henry continued. "I will allow you this once to explain the situation in its entirety before dispensing any judgment."

There was a moment of thoughtful hesitation before Abe spoke. Mercy listened as Abe explained their journey as innocently as it had occurred, right up until they'd discovered the redcoats. Then the two of them took turns explaining their thoughts and actions, how the redcoats had responded, and David's musket shot, closing with the uneventful march back to camp.

Mercy waited in nauseating trepidation as Henry carefully pondered their story. She wasn't afraid of his anger; she was afraid of his disappointment. He was her papa now, and she wanted to always make him proud.

At last, Henry let out a sigh and began. "This world has done you children a disservice; it isn't right that yours is as volatile a world as this. What happened this afternoon ought not to have happened; children should be free to comb the woods and hills without having to make such decisions as these. But alas, this is the world you've been born into, and as such, you must learn to navigate it with prudence, or you will not survive it.

"Those soldiers are meaningless in comparison to your own lives, and you've risked your lives foolishly. Not only your own lives, but your brother David's as well. They are but mere foot soldiers, and even a severe interrogation will produce little fruitful information. The only measurable outcome being a good laugh at the king's expense. However, if your lives would have been lost, the loss would be a greater harm than I believe Abigail or myself could bear. Mercy," he said.

She met his gaze through burning tears.

"Abigail trusted you to make wise decisions, to understand danger and weigh the value of life, and choose the greater. What do we fight for if not a brighter future for you?" he said.

Again, she hung her head.

"I believe your intentions were good, and only your judgment erred. I know you would not have acted recklessly if you'd understood the situation fully, nor do I believe you would put your brothers in such danger willfully. In light of that, I see no need for punishment, only reflection and an apology to your brother David, and Abigail. Both of you should have listened to your younger brother; today, he was the wiser."

"Yes, sir," Abe said.

Mercy couldn't speak, she trudged the few feet between them and planted her face in his chest, sobbing.

"There, there," Henry said, wrapping his arms around her. "We've got you all back in one piece. I'm sure there will be many a good laugh around the fires tonight on account of you capturing those redcoats. You're still the same Mercy who wouldn't let that catfish go, not even when it cost you your finest dress." He lifted her chin. "A memory I will cherish, always."

"Are you cross?" she sniffled.

Henry sighed again. "No. I'm not cross. I simply need you to be wise, and careful. I still have night terrors about that day I almost lost you on Breed's Hill."

"But I saved Mr. Hadley . . ."

"Yes, you did, though I'm not so sure the cost would have been worth it."

"Mr. Henry!" Mercy exclaimed.

"I jest," Henry laughed. "He's a fine man, and a better friend. Now, run after your brother, and apologize like I told you before you forget everything I've said."

Mercy gave him one more hug, before starting after Abe.

"Lord, help me," Henry sighed.

That evening as Mercy washed linens down at the stream with the other ladies in camp, she overheard Abigail gossiping.

"That's right, Mrs. McKinney, Mercy marched those redcoats all the way up here in not but their breeches; had the poor devils fearing for their very lives. That owl of hers was glaring at 'em as though he'd pluck out their eyes if they looked sideways. Henry said that one of them believed she was a witch and swore up and down she'd put a spell on them," Abigail chuckled.

"I'd have thought the same if I hadn't seen the two of them together as oft' as I have," Mrs. Bell said. "It's a peculiar thing, a girl and a bird, but it's harmless."

"At any rate, it sounds like you've got your hands full, Abigail," Mrs. McKinney said.

"Gratefully so," Abigail replied. "Though I've given them two weeks with no wanderin' and no foolishness to think it over."

"They ought to make Mercy a captain," Mrs. Bell said. "Lord knows she's captured more redcoats this month than Washington."

Mercy let out of soft snort, and looked away quickly before anyone could see her blush. Why, there was no way she could be a captain, she was too young . . .

"Two weeks is a long time," David grumbled, as he sat on a crate outside the medical tent.

"It's already been one, Dave. Abigail just wants to make sure we don't run off and do something foolish again," Mercy said.

"I don't see why I've been punished, I tried telling the two of you, but you were too daft to listen," David complained again.

"I'm sorry, Dave," Mercy sighed. "I don't think you're being punished, we are, and you can't go anywhere without us."

"Nathaniel and Mable went swimming with Adelaide over an hour ago, and here we are, slaving away doing extra chores. . . . Why does Theo get to go swimming?" David whined.

"He's taken a liking to Adelaide, and unlike us, he didn't get punished."

"I wish I was an owl," David said. "That bird lives better than the king."

"Probably," Mercy mused.

"Uh oh, here comes Mama!" Abe said.

"Quick, get back to splitting that kindling!" Mercy said, darting back into the medical tent.

A few moments later, Abigail entered the tent carrying a basket of new bandages. "Looks like David is working himself into a lather working on that kindling," she said in satisfaction.

"I think he's a little sore the Bells got to go swimming today and he had to stay back and work," Mercy replied.

"Good, that means the lesson's sticking," Abigail said. "And as for you, I want you to change the dressings on these boys here and boil the old ones. I saw Abe working his hands raw splitting more wood for the fires, so it looks like you'll have to draw your own water."

"Yes, ma'am," Mercy groaned.

Mercy swapped the bandages with care, as she moved up and down the rows of patients under Abigail's watchful eye. She felt bad for her brothers, suffering on her account. Deep down she knew this was Abigail's way of showing love. Abigail's aim was to see to it that they all survived the war, healthy and sound, as far as it depended on her, and Mercy's poor decision had jeopardized that goal.

Carrying the basket of soiled bandages out to the cauldron, she sat it down and straightened her back. She eyed the empty pail mournfully, the stream was a fair walk from there, and it took several pails full to get the water deep enough to boil the bandages.

"Would you like a hand, Miss Young?"

Mercy turned to see Lt. Davis standing a few feet behind her.

"I can do it," Mercy said, looking away in embarrassment. She felt like a little child being punished . . . Lt. Davis probably thought she was so irresponsible. Picking up the pail, she started for the stream, about halfway there she heard footfalls behind her trotting to catch up. Looking over her shoulder, she saw Lt. Davis with his own pail catching up to her.

"I said I could get it on my own," Mercy mumbled.

"I know," Lt. Davis said. "But you've been doing such fine work lately, there's little for me to do in my own medical tent."

Mercy didn't reply as she stooped over to fill her pail.

"She loves you, Mercy," Lt. Davis said, filling his own pail. "Even though she's punished you, she's proud of you, surely you must know that."

"I do," Mercy said, straightening.

"And I'm proud of you too," he said. "The whole camp is."

Her heart pulsed boldly at his remark; she hadn't expected him to say that. Maybe she hadn't soiled her reputation after all.

"Thank you, sir," Mercy said, turning back towards the camp, a slight smile tugging at the corners of her mouth.

It took several more trips, but eventually the cauldron was full, the fire burning, and the rags added. Lt. Davis was called away with Abigail to help deliver a baby, leaving Mercy alone to her work. Maybe things hadn't turned out so bad after all. Lt. Davis hadn't seemed to have lessened his opinion of her, and perhaps others hadn't as well.

Chapter 8

Mercy awoke on the morning of July 6th to the call to arms; the camp was already a flurry of humanity by the time she emerged from the wagon. Meeting Abigail and Adelaide outside, they raced for the medical tent, leaving the children in the care of Mrs. Bell.

"What's going on?" Mercy asked.

"I don't know, child," Abigail replied. "Maybe those red devils have finally decided to have at us, Lord have mercy!"

Lt. Davis met them at the medical tent, already harnessing teams of horses to the flatbeds.

"What's the word?" Abigail asked.

"Help me with the horses," Lt. Davis said. "The redcoats under General Burgoyne himself have taken Fort Ticonderoga just this morning and are pushing south on the heels of General St. Claire. General Washington has ordered us to be ready to evacuate if Howe moves against our position in response to their victory. It appears Burgoyne is trying to cut us off."

"Lord, help us," Abigail said, reaching for a harness.

"Are there any redcoats left in England?" Mercy asked, perplexed. "How can there be so many?"

"God only knows," Lt. Davis said. "General Burgoyne is pressing with almost nine thousand and there's another fifteen thousand in New York, and Hessians as well."

"Is there no help for us?" Abigail said, looking to the sky.

Once the teams were harnessed, the ladies saw to the needs of their patents anxiously awaiting the British advance. But as the hours wore on, no attack came. Dispatches arrived, communicating General Burgoyne had called off his pursuit of General St. Claire and returned to Fort Ticonderoga. General Howe, the British commander in New York, surprisingly, made no advance.

General St. Claire was recalled by General Washington to answer for surrendering the fort. Grumblings for his court martial were already percolating through the camp. The loss of Fort Ticonderoga meant the British now controlled access to the Hudson River Valley, a river highway from Canada to the city of New York. This put Washington and the Continentals in a desperate situation once again and made a way for the British to cut off New England from the rest of the colonies.

Complaints arose concerning General Washington as well. Many Americans were beginning to believe he was incapable of beating the British, and even Congress was pressuring him to do something in spite of the British having all the advantages. The king had more soldiers, his army was better supplied, they possessed a real navy, and had the support of the Tories. Washington's army was always hanging by a thread, in need of food and supplies, even items as simple as shoes as many of the soldiers marched barefoot. Mercy prayed for him; his had to be the loneliest and hardest of all positions.

As the day drew to a close, many long faces passed her on her way back to their wagon, further evidence of the damage done to morale due to the loss of Fort Ticonderoga. Benjamin and Henry would not be returning tonight, their unit was ordered to remain on the hilltops overlooking the British in New York in case General Howe decided to march against them during the night.

The Bells and Youngs sat eating firecakes by firelight on account no one was allowed to leave camp to go foraging or fishing during the day. Even the younger boys ate their cakes in silence, the melancholy of the camp had not been lost on them. The flavorless food accurately summed up the mood as they wrestled it down their throats.

"Hey," Mercy said. "What if we played a game?"

"A game?" David asked.

"Yes. I'll think of a creature, and you all try and guess what it is," Mercy said.

Nathaniel looked to Mrs. Bell, who frowned, but didn't reply.

"Okay," Mercy said. "I've got it."

"It's probably your owl," Abe said, rolling his eyes.

"No," Mercy said. "It has fur, not feathers, and it's hardly bigger than a shoe."

"A hare!" Mable said.

"Close," Mercy said. "It has a long fluffy tail."

"A squirrel?" David asked.

"That's it, David. I was thinking of a squirrel!" Mercy said. "Now you give it a try."

"Hmmm, okay, I've got one. It's big—"

"A horse!" Abe said.

"No, not so big as a horse," David said.

"Well, how am I supposed to know what you mean when you say big?" Abe complained.

"How indeed," Mrs. Bell muttered.

"It's big like the cauldron Mercy is always stirring, and black too, and scary," David replied.

"A bear!" Abe exclaimed.

"Yes! It was a bear. I get the shivers just thinking about them," David said.

"Okay. Abe, now it's your turn," Mercy said.

"Give me a moment, I know an awful lot of critters," Abe said.

"You can't take all night, Abe. I want another try," David complained.

"Okay, okay, I've got one," Abe said. "It's a hunter."

"A coywolf!" David exclaimed.

"No. It sits real still and waits for its food to come to it."

"A spider?" Mercy said.

"No, not a spider. It doesn't have fur, or feathers either."

"A snake?" Mable asked.

"How big is it?" Nathaniel asked.

"Hmmm," Abe said. "A good sized one would fill a mug."

"What kind of hunter is that small?" David asked.

"It lives in the water . . ."

"A fish?" Mable guessed.

"No. It also lives on land."

"A frog!" Mrs. Bell blurted, immediately throwing her hands over her mouth in embarrassment.

"Mrs. Bell?!" Abe complained. "You can't guess! You're a grown woman."

Abigail burst out laughing as Mrs. Bell lowered her hands. "I was going to say it if you didn't," Abigail gasped.

"I'm sorry, Abraham. I—I don't know what came over me," Mrs. Bell said, perplexed.

"I do," Abigail said. "It's good fun, Mrs. Bell."

"It's a frog," Mable said.

"Yes, Mable," Abe sighed. "You guessed it, it's a frog."

"Is it my turn?" Mable asked.

"Yes, Mable, give it a go," Mercy said.

"It's tiny, and—"

"A mouse!" David said.

"Dave!" Mable growled. "I didn't even get to say two words!"

"It's alright, Mable. You can give it another go," Mercy said.

"Says who?!" David snapped. "I guessed it."

"I think we should give Mrs. Bell a try," Abigail said. "She did discover a creature after all."

"No, Abigail. I—I shouldn't . . ."

"Give it a try, Mama," Mable said.

"Yes," Adelaide nodded.

Mrs. Bell looked around at all the hopeful faces. "Well, maybe just once wouldn't hurt anything . . ."

"Surely not," Abigail agreed.

"Alright, let me see. I don't know as many of God's creatures as Abraham, and I find many of them quite detestable. Okay, I've chosen one of my favorites."

"A robin?" Mable guessed.

"No, but it is small, perhaps even frail. How it begins is not so lovely, but the end is splendid and beautiful."

Mercy watched the firelight dance in a dozen inquisitive eyes as they listened. They'd forgotten the day, the loss of Fort

Ticonderoga, the difficult odds they faced again and again. She didn't know where the notion had come from, but was glad it'd come, a brief respite, a moment of simple joy.

"It comes in the warm spring months, and stays through the summer, but as it grows cold, there are none to be found. It never does anyone any harm and enjoys flowers as much as my sweet Adelaide."

"A butterfly," Mercy said.

"Yes," smiled Mrs. Bell. "A beautiful butterfly."

"They're one of my favorites too," Mercy said.

"And mine," agreed Abigail.

"Wish they didn't start out as worms, though," Mrs. Bell said.

"Perhaps it's because God wanted us not to judge someone based on how they begin, but rather on who they're striving to be," Abigail said.

"Perhaps," replied Mrs. Bell. "But not every worm becomes a butterfly. Sometimes, worms . . . are just worms."

After a couple more rounds of the game, the Bells bid the Youngs goodnight. As Mercy lay writing in her diary by candlelight, she thought about what Mrs. Bell had said. Mercy had met plenty of wonderful people since Lexington, and she'd also met some terrible ones. At first, she'd believed Mrs. Bell was a worm, but now . . . now she saw her as a butterfly. A strict, stiff, monochromatic butterfly.

Even some of the redcoats and Hessians who'd fallen under her care turned out to be more butterfly than worm. Simply men, under orders, many miles from home. Prisoners like her father, awaiting a prisoner exchange, or worse, the end of the war. Everyone a captive of circumstances of which they had little say or control.

The following morning, Mercy was asked to join Lt. Davis on a supply run to Philadelphia. She'd been on many such runs, but never to the capital city. Abigail had been asked first but declined due to her lack of appreciation for long wagon trips. Lt. Davis had only made one condition; Theo had to stay home.

They'd left while the sky was still gray in the wee hours of the morning. The air still held its damp chill, and the birds had not yet awakened as the wheels of their flatbed clattered over the rugged road. The morning was as plain and ordinary as any she could remember, still, things could change so fast in her volatile world, a notion that wouldn't allow her to be at ease.

Though they were in Continental territory, Lt. Davis kept ever vigilant. Tories were everywhere, and constantly caused trouble for the rebels. They were seemingly ordinary citizens, who remained loyal to the king, and aided by their disguise, sought occasion to hamper the Patriots in any way they could.

The journey would take them twelve hours round trip, besides the time to load the supplies. Twelve hours without changing bandages, boiling bandages, drying bandages, nothing to do with bandages. No siblings, no chores, no responsibilities of any kind. It was as good as a day off and an adventure all rolled into one. And she planned to enjoy herself.

"How are you fairing, Mercy?" Lt. Davis asked.

"Well, sir. Even when I am tempted to complain, all I need do is look about the medical tent and remember I have it much better than they do."

"That was a nasty bout with the pox, especially to lose some of the little ones. Illness shows no mercy," Lt. Davis said.

"We saved many as well," Mercy replied.

"That is why I need good nurses like you, to remind me to dwell on our victories rather than our defeats."

"Well, I aim to dwell on this beautiful day, and let those in the medical tent dwell on the medical tent," Mercy said.

"You're right again. I shouldn't spoil an opportunity for rest with talk of our labors."

"Lt. Davis, do you like butterflies?"

The young lieutenant straightened in the buckboard. "Well, I don't know . . . I doubt I've given a butterfly a passing thought in years," he said, pondering her question. "I suppose I do, they're not a pest, nor do they sting, and they do add a delicate bit of color to the world."

"Would you fancy yourself a worm or a butterfly?" Mercy asked.

"I am quite certain that I am human," Lt. Davis replied.

"I know, but Abigail said that we should not judge people based on where they begin, like the worm that turns into a butterfly, but Mrs. Bell replied that not all worms become butterflies, some worms are simply worms."

"Ahh, they were referring to character. Though I would counter that even worms have their own glorious purpose given by their Creator. And if looked at in the correct light, they are all magnificent."

"You would complicate a simple question," Mercy grumbled.

"I'm a doctor, it's my nature to examine everything."

"Humph," Mercy replied.

"Which do you think I am?" he asked.

It was Mercy's turn to straighten. "Well, I was going to say butterfly, but now I'm sure you must be one of those magnificent worms," she replied snidely.

Lt. Davis grinned, shaking his head. "I'm glad to see you haven't lost any of your fire."

Chapter 9

Philadelphia was everything Mercy had dreamed of sitting elegantly astride the Delaware River. The city was modern and its layout clean. The roads were straight, lined with beautiful large houses, but the jewel of the city was Independence Hall. It was a massive two–story red brick building, with a dazzling white belfry, adorned with the largest bell Mercy had ever seen.

All around them ladies in fine dresses, and men in white wigs went about their business. Mercy felt out of place and comely around so many well–to–do women, most of them so absorbed with their gossip, they didn't even pay her any mind.

"It's a might different than the camp," Lt. Davis said, noting her discomfort.

"I feel as though we're riding through a fairytale," Mercy said.

"Much of it is," Lt. Davis said. "Many of these folks are deep in debt, some have sold their own children to keep up appearances."

"What?!" Mercy asked, perplexed.

"Aristocracy is a difficult thing to surrender I'm afraid. When one has built up an image and identity of wealth and success, the shame of losing it becomes unbearable. My family runs in these circles. Dances, parties, and duty, all the finer things. I'm afraid I've been quite the disappointment."

"Do you miss it?"

"I've found that I prefer the genuine society of common folk, as opposed to the endless masquerade of high society. It is much less exhausting to know whom one is conversing with under the mask."

"Do you know any of these folks?" Mercy asked.

"Many," Lt. Davis said. "The looks of contempt are not for your sake, but mine. I showed such promise . . ." he sighed.

"You still show great promise."

"Yes, well, I'm not alone. Many of our leadership have also greatly disappointed. Benjamin Franklin may be at the top of the list. If the redcoats are able to take this city, the Tories will not rest until they've rid it of all who've sided with the rebellion. They will hang us all if they can catch us."

"But certainly, you must have some friends amongst them?"

"Duty triumphs over everything, I'm afraid," Lt. Davis said.

At last, they pulled up outside a white two–story building which had been converted into a medical facility. Lt. Davis jumped down from the wagon, wrapping the reigns around a hitching post, before coming round to Mercy's side and helping her down out of the buckboard.

"Wait here for a moment while I meet with the quartermaster," Lt. Davis said.

Mercy meandered to the horses, scratching them here and there as they swatted flies away with their tails. The city seemed so bright and prosperous, but even as she watched the goings on, she could sense the divided loyalties of individuals as they passed, either acknowledging one another or refusing to do so; friends, who up until recently, had attended the same parties, now silently at war with one another. Some were no doubt related by marriage both distantly and not so distant.

Mercy took a bite of an apple Abigail had sent along and then fed the rest to one of the horses. Presently a nurse about Mercy's age, perhaps a little older, walked out of the infirmary carrying a large basin. She walked a few feet into the yard, before dumping the pinkish contents onto the lawn. Seeing Mercy, she nodded, and Mercy returned the gesture.

Then a smile of recognition spread over the girl's face. "Mercy? Mercy Young, is that you?"

"Yes," Mercy answered, searching her memory.

The nurse removed her bonnet and rushed towards the wagon as recognition dawned.

"Maddie Smith?" Mercy asked.

The girl met her, her bright blue eyes flashing, and her freckled cheeks bunched up in a smile. "Yes!" Maddie exclaimed. "My goodness, Mercy, you've changed so much I hardly recognized you!"

"I didn't recognize you either," Mercy said, giving her a hug. "What are you doing here?!"

"I could ask you the same!" Maddie said, releasing her. "Mama's been worried sick about the four of you since you ran off that night back in Lexington."

Mercy gasped. "I'm real sorry about that, we had to leave, we needed to find Papa."

"And did you?"

"He was sent to England." Mercy frowned.

"Oh, Mercy . . ." Maddie gasped covering her mouth with her hands. "Why didn't you ever come home?"

"We've been staying with a sweet couple who own the tavern in Cambridge. They haven't got any children of their own, but they see us as the Lord's blessing. We've had it good," Mercy replied.

"Mama will be glad to hear it. She can finally put her worry to rest."

"What about you?" Mercy asked. "What are you doing so far from Lexington?"

"Papa got shot," Maddie said. "But he's alright now . . . though he lost his leg. He was sent here to recover, and Mama just couldn't sit still, so we all came. Mama and I now work at the infirmary, and Papa and Samuel work as smithies here in Philadelphia."

"I'm sorry," Mercy said.

"Don't be. Better to lose a leg than a papa."

Lt. Davis returned while they were talking and gave Maddie a courteous bow before addressing Mercy. "I hate to disrupt your conversing, but I'm afraid we must make haste if we are to return to camp before nightfall."

"It's alright," Maddie said. "I should be getting back before Mama comes looking for me. It was good to see you, Mercy, hopefully we can visit again soon." Maddie gave them a parting curtsy and returned to the infirmary.

"The quartermaster will meet us at the back of the infirmary and help us load our supplies," Lt. Davis said, unhitching the horses.

Mercy climbed into the buckboard and Lt. Davis guided the team around the building to the back door. After the crates of supplies were loaded, Lt. Davis stopped at the tavern for some boiled eggs to eat on their journey home, and they were off.

Mercy felt a burden lifted that she hadn't known she still carried. Mrs. Smith would now know the truth of what had become of them and would be able to sleep easier tonight. In hindsight, it would have been a piece of mercy to have left her a note or something. Lord knows a woman in her position already had plenty of other worries.

They were nearly halfway between Philadelphia and the camp when the sky began to grow untimely dark. A cool wind rustled the leaves of the forest trees lining the road, fluttering her dress and blowing Mercy's hair across her face. Then the first icy droplets began to fall.

"Blast these dreadful storms. I can't remember a season in my life with so much rain. No sooner has the mud begun to dry than another storm drenches the whole of the colonies again," Lt. Davis fumed.

He snapped the reigns, causing the horses to pick up the pace, but it was no use. Thunder rumbled in the distance as churning clouds continued to darken. Large droplets of rain began pelting the wagon, forming dark polka dots on Mercy's navy–blue dress.

Lt. Davis looked at her with a mournful expression. Lightning flashed brilliantly overhead followed by a frightful BOOM, and the sky opened up. Sheets of icy rain driven by a ferocious wind blasted the wagon. Lt. Davis threw his coat around Mercy and drove the team off the road and under the dense leaves of the forest trees. Pulling the brake, he jumped down and ran around to help Mercy.

Together they ducked under the flatbed to wait out the storm.

"Will the supplies be alright?" Mercy shouted over the tumult.

"A few things like bandages will need to be dried out, but the majority should be alright. I'm sorry I've gotten you into this mess," Lt. Davis hollered back.

"We've been in worse," Mercy replied.

Lt. Davis nodded, reflecting on the night on Dorchester Heights. "Still, I have no doubt I shall receive a look of rebuke from Abigail when we arrive, as though I could control the weather."

"Probably," Mercy said. "She's a mother hen. Though it's Mrs. Bell who'll say, 'I told you they should have gone with a chaperone, just think of the impropriety, two young people gallivanting around after dark,'" Mercy said in her best Mrs. Bell voice.

"Yeah," Lt. Davis chuffed. "Though I had not intended us to arrive after dark. Mrs. Bell is not wrong in her defense of propriety, believe me when I tell you that integrity and good character once lost is a difficult thing to recover."

"Just be glad you hadn't taken Adelaide. Mrs. Bell would likely have you in the stocks if you had not arrived before dark."

"Let's pray the storm passes quickly," Lt. Davis said. "The days are long this time of year; we may still make it in time."

Thankfully, the storm did pass quickly. Lt. Davis laid his coat on the buckboard for Mercy to sit on and pulled the wagon back onto the leaf littered road. The hardened ruts were now soft again, a fortunate blessing that their trip would be smoother from here on out. A hazy steam swirled above the road as midafternoon rays began the process of drying the world out once more.

Twice along the road, trees had fallen on account of the high winds and soft soil and Lt. Davis was forced to unharness the team and use them to drag the debris from their path so their journey could continue. Mercy admired him, he seemed wise beyond his twenty years, and as caring as any man she'd met. His fine clothes were a mess of leaves, twigs, and mud by the time he'd reharnessed the team after clearing the second tree.

The sun had dipped low in the hills to the west as the wagon came in view of the camp. The team had dutifully overcome every obstacle and Lt. Davis promised he'd make sure they received plenty of fodder, and an apple each for their fine work. As Mercy expected, Abigail waited anxiously for them at the medical tent and was nearly beside herself at the sight of Lt. Davis.

"Lord, bless you," she said. "That was an awful storm. Are the two of you alright?"

"We're fine, Mama," Mercy said, giving her a hug. "Lt. Davis kept me in excellent care, we were never in any danger."

"Thank you," Abigail said, turning to him.

"Let's get these things unloaded, and the bandages drying before they mold," Lt. Davis said. "Then it's time for a hot bath."

Abigail nodded, and together with Adelaide's help, the wagon was unloaded and sorted, and the bandages hung on a line near the fire to dry. Adelaide looked at Mercy with anticipation as they placed the last crate, anxious to hear the story of their adventure. It was certainly a day worth recording in her diary.

Chapter 10

July 29, 1777

Today the most elegantly dressed, vigorously courteous, and funniest talking man I have ever seen rode into camp astride a magnificent white horse. I had to hear his name four times to remember it and I'm still not sure I got it right. His name is Marie Joseph Paul Yves Roch Gilbert du Montier de La Fayette, or as General Washington seems satisfied to call him, Marquis de Lafayette.

He arrived in Philadelphia on the 27th and has already been given the rank of Major General, although he is but nineteen. Henry says it doesn't look like he has ever shaved, but he's a Frenchman, a well–connected one at that, and we desperately need their support. Henry also said that he has volunteered to serve without pay if Congress would only give him the chance to fight the redcoats.

Many of the younger ladies in camp have found themselves quite taken with him. He is the object of all the gossip since his arrival; Lt. Davis says *he's nothing more than a French peacock. It could be there is a touch of jealousy, though I've never known Lt. Davis to fret about such trivial things.*

Henry and Ben's riflemen have been ordered north to support General Gates near Saratoga; he is preparing to meet General Burgoyne marching south from Fort Ticonderoga. Fortunately, Lt. Davis and his aides have also been ordered north as the fighting there may be some of the worst. It seems the British have finally agreed on a strategy to cut off New England from the colonies: General Burgoyne sweeping down the Hudson River Valley to join up with Howe in New York, before pressing on to Philadelphia.

Henry says it is our duty for the sake of the cause to weather this storm. Every day we survive costs the king precious resources, tipping the scales of victory slowly in our favor. The majority of our patients have been sent to Philadelphia; it gives me solace to know they will be in Maddie's care. Maddie is a far gentler soul than I, the soldiers recovering there are likely to be spoiled.

At first light we will rise, harness the horses, and be off. Only the Good Lord knows if we will ever pass this way again. The summer fighting season is already drawing to a close, neither side can afford to go into the winter without a victory, we are surely driving into the head of the storm.

Mercy Young, 14 years old

The morning's light found the Youngs in the middle of a wagon train heading north towards Saratoga. Henry's riflemen and a cavalry unit would provide security for the day long journey. Adelaide had received her mother's blessing to go along with the Youngs as a member of Lt. Davis's team.

As Ben drove, Mercy and Abigail knitted in the swaying wagon, while the boys played a battle with lead soldiers. Adelaide, however, chose to ride next to Ben. He and Henry had been away more than they'd been around the past few months, scouting and foraging, simply trying to figure out why the redcoats were hesitating. Mercy didn't mind though, most days she had Adelaide all to herself, and now that she was staying with them, they would have even more time.

"Is that a Bible's width?" Abe asked out of the blue.

Mercy looked up just in time to see Adelaide slide a few inches further away on the buckboard.

"Oh, let them alone, Abraham," Abigail chided. "I've got my eye on them."

"Mrs. Bell entrusted *me* to keep an eye on them, Mrs. Abigail," Abe countered. "She said you'd be too soft."

Abigail blushed. "Well, consider yourself relieved of duty, young man. This is *my* wagon, and it'll be *my* rules we're followin'."

"Alright, but she instructed me to report any questionable behavior, Mrs. Abigail."

"Since when did she take such a liking to you?" muttered Abigail.

"Since I've been making great strides," Abe replied confidently. "That's what she told me. I'm shaping up into a fine young man."

"It appears we have a spy in our midst," Abigail mused.

"They hang spies," Ben called out matter–of–factly.

"As they should," Abigail said.

Abe fidgeted under her gaze. "Perhaps I could manage to let this one infraction pass," he said. "Not all Bibles are of the same width after all."

"That's a sensible lad," Abigail agreed.

Abe smiled sheepishly and went back to his battle with David.

Abigail shook her head. "Imagine, a woman having her own son turn on her . . ."

"It's not that, Mama," Mercy said. "Abe is a glutton for duty."

"Not the worst trait a man can possess, I suppose," Abigail surrendered. "Though I'd prefer loyalty."

Mercy sorted. "Yes, that would probably serve the moment better."

As the sun rose, the temperature under the wagon canvas rose. The boys wearied of their battle and began antagonizing one another. Mercy and Abigail took turns coming up with ideas to help them overcome the monotony of the journey, but their best efforts only lasted an hour at the most.

"Can't this weather make up its mind?" Abigail groaned. "Rainin' and stormin' one moment, and hot as a forge the next; air so thick you could cut it with a knife, only suitable living conditions for these hordes of biting flies and mosquitos. Of which there's no escape except to stand near the smoke of a hot fire. If only Adam and Eve had had the good sense to leave that dreadful tree alone."

"Awe, Mama," David said. "You have to learn to look on the bright side, with all this rain, Abe and I've been able to have terrific ship races in the streams in the wagon ruts. And Mr. Henry said if it rains much more, there'll be fish swimming right down the road. Wouldn't that be a sight to see!"

Mercy felt for Abigail as she blinked at David and tried to reply.

"Yes, David. You're right, I should be counting my blessings."

A familiar crack of a musket towards the rear of the column sent them all diving for cover. It was followed by another, and then several more. Then there was whooping and hollering coming from the trees lining the road behind them. More muskets fired as a smoky haze rose from the ranks of riflemen forming the rear guard.

A cavalry rider rode up the column, stopping momentarily at each wagon. "Best get the women and children to lie down in the back, and get your musket ready, son," the soldier said to Ben.

"Is it the Tories?" Ben asked.

"No," the rider replied. "Iroquois!" Then he rode on to the next wagon.

"Oh, good heavens!" Abigail exclaimed, cupping her hand over her mouth.

Adelaide scrambled into the back, and they did their best to lay low. Ben kept the team moving forward with the reigns in one hand and his rifle in the other.

The sounds of whooping war cries and musket fire continued up the column towards them, the smoke and smell of spent powder saturated the air.

"Lord help us!" Abigail pleaded as she lay, holding David close.

"Abe!" Ben hollered. "It's getting close, take my rifle and watch out the back. If you see one, just shoot nice and easy they way Mr. Hadley taught you."

"Okay," Abe said bravely as he clambered over the girls to get to the front.

Taking Ben's rifle, he made his way to the back of the wagon and took a seat, resting the muzzle on the backboard. Mercy watched with bated breath as he swiveled the rife back and forth searching the tree line. Adelaide reached through the tangle of belongings, taking Mercy's hand. The sound of the nearing battle was dreadful.

Smoke and shot, the smell of sulfur, screams and whoops, fear and panic . . . then, quiet.

As suddenly as it had started, the fighting stopped except for a few sporadic rifle shots. Abe relaxed the hammer on Ben's rifle and pulled it back into the wagon. One by one, Abigail and the Youngs sat up, looking back in the direction the ambush had taken place. Slowly the smoke began to clear and several more wagons and militiamen came into view.

Another rider rode up the line asking for Abigail. Slowing to walk beside their wagon, he explained that three riflemen had been wounded, and Lt. Davis was seeking their assistance. Mercy and Adelaide agreed to go and leave Abigail with David who still trembled in the bed of the wagon. Climbing down, they followed the rider towards the end of the column.

As they neared the end, Mercy noticed a half–naked dark–skinned man with a mohawk and war paint lying beside the road, nearly pale with shock as he gripped a bleeding thigh. At first, she thought he was terrifying, but as she looked again, she recognized the terror in his eyes. She'd seen it in the eyes of so many of her patients before.

Without thinking, she left the road, starting towards the man.

"Hey, Miss!" the rider called, turning his horse to face her. "We don't treat the savages."

"But—"

"They're animals," the rider snarled.

Mercy looked back at the man who'd just lost consciousness. He was different, true, but also the same. "But we help the *redcoats?*"

"They're human," the rider responded, turning his horse away.

Mercy looked at Adelaide, who shook her head sorrowfully and followed the rider. Taking one last look at the painted man, Mercy turned away, her heart feeling heavy.

A short distance later they arrived at a flatbed wagon where Lt. Davis was already working on the riflemen. The driver slowed the wagon for a moment to let the girls board before slapping the reins. It wasn't safe to stop.

Mercy set to work on the first man she came to. He'd suffered a deep knife gash across his chest, but it hadn't gone deep enough to cause any life–threatening injuries. Grabbing a rag, she poured water on it and began dabbing the wound clean. The man, old enough to be her father, groaned but didn't cry out. Once it was clean, she laid a fresh bandage over the wound and wrapped it tightly to the man's chest.

"Thank you, Miss," the soldier grunted, laying himself down.

"You're welcome."

"You girls alright?" Lt. Davis asked, finishing with his patient.

"Fine, sir," Adelaide replied.

"Dreadful creatures," Lt. Davis said. "Though I believe they only meant to frighten us."

Chapter 11

On August 3rd, word arrived in General Gates' camp that a siege had begun on a Continental fort called Fort Stanwix, an outpost in the Mohawk River Valley some eighty miles to their west. The besieging army was largely made up of Loyalist Tory militia and natives allied to the British. The fort was holding its own but would need relief if they were to survive. Losing the fort would be another crippling blow to the Continentals and would put the British one step closer to their goal of cutting off New England.

General Gates formed a relief party of about eight hundred militia to rescue their surrounded countrymen. Benjamin and Henry would be going as part of the light rifleman unit under a German American named General Herkimer, who'd won himself a reputation during the French and Indian war. Herkimer could speak German, English, and Mohawk, and was well respected for his wise leadership amongst his men. The relief was ordered to march out as soon as they were ready.

Unlike New York, there was no shortage of trouble this far north. The landscape was infinitely more primitive, and natives allied to the British took every opportunity to harass the Continental forces and their allies with demoralizing effect. In the current circumstances, Mercy found it difficult to will her mind to sleep, knowing the natives often attacked without warning or provocation, and spared neither woman nor child.

This was a wild place, and even as she worked, she felt as though eyes were watching her from the trees. Theo seemed to sense it too, his head ever turning about, his feet restless, constantly shifting on her shoulder. Lt. Davis told her that the natives fear owls, and view them as a bad omen, an omen of death. She hoped their superstition would offer her some protection, and she kept him with her always.

No one left the camp, the boys never wandered far in their search for firewood, nor tarried where they were not in sight of the sentries. The eeriness played tricks on Mercy's mind; often she would think she saw someone, only to look again and no one was there. It was a heaviness, like the anxious fear of monsters lurking in the dark.

Mercy regretted ever complaining about the monotony of their life in Middle Brook; she vowed she'd never again groan about the boredom of peace. Nor would she complain of having to confront redcoats, who marched in formation wearing bright colors for all to see. Their new enemy often didn't wear much at all and could attack and then escape without ever being seen.

"Are you alright?" Lt. Davis asked, causing Mercy to jump.

"I don't like it here," Mercy confessed. "It's awfully unsettling; I fear when I wake, and more so when I sleep."

Lt. Davis nodded. "It is a mysterious place, as wild as the savages who inhabit it."

"Why do you call them that?" Mercy asked.

"Everyone calls them that. It's what they are, savages, without conscience or fear of God. They're more animal than man."

"They look like men to me," Mercy said. "Different, but I figure that's just their way. They've had to adapt and live in this wild place; it makes sense they'd also seem wild."

"But they behave like animals," Lt. Davis replied.

"If that's the only requirement, then my brothers are also animals," Mercy replied. "Perhaps they'd behave like men if they were treated like men?"

"I fear you will find few who share your sentiment," he said. "They've butchered people, good decent folks, who wanted no part of this war."

"We haven't treated them any better. Henry said we raided and burned their villages in South Carolina just as they burned and raided ours . . . we left one to die on the road on our way here. If he'd been a redcoat, we'd have placed him on the flatbed and given him care. I saw through his painted face the same fear I've seen dozens of times before. The fear of a *man* who didn't want to die."

"What are you saying?" Lt. Davis asked.

"I'm saying that we treat them with the same malice they treat us, only we justify our own actions while condemning theirs. Leaving him to die is no less barbarous than killing innocent folks, both actions are savage and without mercy. Having left that man there . . . I should expect no greater care from them should they take me, and it is that which haunts me," Mercy said.

"Mercy is an apt name," Lt. Davis sighed. "If more of us thought like you, perhaps wars could be avoided entirely. I have no doubt that after some reflection, my own mind will come to see them differently. I am sorry my blind indifference has caused you so much unrest. My conscience has indeed been pricked, and I find my argument has been rooted in ignorance, based solely on appearances, and as such, is baseless. Thank you for sharing your heart."

Mercy nodded, grateful for his response, yet slightly embarrassed over lecturing a grown man.

"I will have your wagon moved nearer to the fires. Perhaps it will help you sleep more soundly tonight," he said. Lt. Davis tipped his hat and started in the direction of his quarters.

Mercy scanned the wood line one more time before picking up her pail and heading for the stream. She looked away only for a moment to dip it into the water before withdrawing it and scanning her surroundings again. She felt like a mouse just waiting for the cat to pounce.

***

"Mercy!" Lt. Davis shouted, running towards her from the medical tent.

It had been four days since Henry and Benjamin left with General Herkimer to relieve Fort Stanwix. Yesterday around midafternoon a storm had blown up and it'd poured rain for several hours. They'd spent half the night sorting wet supplies and drying things out. Just after one in the morning on the 6th, she'd finished her shift and was about to start fixing supper when she heard him.

Looking up in alarm through the smokey beginnings of a wet fire, she braced herself for the worst.

He pulled up, panting. "Mercy," he gasped. "You and Adelaide are needed immediately; Herkimer's boys were ambushed yesterday, before they made the fort. Tories and natives alike set in on them. The general has been wounded, along with hundreds of the other boys, they've been marching through the day and this night to get back, they'll be arriving shortly!"

"Go, Mercy!" Abe said. "I can take care of us."

Adelaide had already climbed down out of the wagon and together they raced after Lt. Davis, mud splashing on their dresses as they went. Reaching the tent, they found Abigail working feverishly to set up as many gurneys as she could. Lt. Davis set to work preparing the surgeon's table, laying out his tools, including the amputation saw.

Mercy could sense the worry written on Abigail's face, she felt it too. There was a commotion outside as the soldiers in the camp rushed to meet the militia and help ferry the wounded to the tent. Putting on a brave face, Mercy nodded to Adelaide as they prepared themselves for the horrors which awaited them.

From the moment the first patient entered the tent, the ladies went to work strategically sorting the ones who could be saved from the ones who couldn't, and then sorting those still further based on their odds of survival, and how immediately they needed care.

General Herkimer, who'd been hit in the leg, was placed on the surgeon's table. He was given a bit of ale before Lt. Davis began probing for the ball. Mercy wanted desperately to search for her brother and adopted father, but the need was too great here. She moved quickly from patient to patient, wrapping wounds, assessing breaks, directing those who couldn't be saved to be brought outside. It was a terrible thing, and the weight of it would always come back to her in the quiet hours of the night.

They kept coming, wounded men and boys, who'd paid dearly for freedom's cause. A chorus of shovels outside joined the sounds of suffering as men prepared to burry those who'd be lost. It was a sound beyond imagination; felt, more than it was heard, in the soul; a mourning of the pitiful plight of man.

"How can we help?" a voice behind her asked.

Turning, she looked up through tear filling eyes into Henry's tired face. Throwing her arms around him she buried her face in his chest.

"We're alright, Mercy. The Good Lord saw to that," he said, squeezing her tight. "Now tell me, how can we be of help?"

Mercy released him, smiling softly to Ben who stood behind him in the narrow aisle. "We could use another team to carry out the ones we can't save to make room for the ones we can," she said.

Henry nodded sorrowfully. "Lead the way."

It wasn't until the following morning, long after the sun had risen in the sky, that weary hands and heavy hearts were able to rest. Fort Stanwix was still under siege; the militia had lost more than four hundred men dead or wounded. The general's leg would likely have to be amputated.

"How were you able to escape?" Abigail asked, slowly sipping a coffee held in exhausted trembling fingers.

"We were nearly to the fort, a place called Oriskany. It happened in a moment. They just appeared, I can't explain it, but they were all around us," Henry said. "It was the perfect ambush. They picked us apart, taking cover behind the trees and shrubs. General Herkimer was hit, and they propped him up against a thick tree on the roadside. I kid you not, he lit up his pipe, and continued to direct the fight. Twice they nearly overran us, but the general kept us in order. Then, just when it seemed we could last no longer, the skies opened up. Sheets of rain fell so heavy a man could hardly see his hand in front of his face.

"The fighting ground to a halt, and the enemy was forced to seek refuge. By the grace of God, we were hidden under the wing of the storm. The general sent a runner for relief from the fort, and by the time the storm lifted, a company from the fort had attacked a Loyalist Indian village, causing the natives to disengage from the battle and race home to defend their loved ones. Without native support, the Tories were at a disadvantage and chose not to continue the struggle. Seizing providence, we made all haste to retreat, our losses being nearly half our strength."

"It was the most horrible fighting I've seen," Ben said. "They leapt upon us with tomahawks and knives, slashing and hacking as our boys tried to defend themselves, swinging their muskets like clubs. How the general kept his wits. . . . He saved us all."

"I'm so sorry, Ben," Adelaide said.

"Will the fort be able to hold?" Abe asked.

"For a time," Henry answered. "General Gates is sure to send more help. I've heard it may even be the brave General Benedict Arnold."

"Enough talk of war, we'd best get some rest," Abigail suggested. "Lt. Davis will need us again in just a few hours to change the dressings."

Chapter 12

Mercy woke the following night to the sound of someone's scuffling feet around their fire. It was late, or perhaps very early in the morning. Lifting the canvas, she was surprised to see Ben sitting on a stump talking quietly with someone. Lifting the canvas still further, she saw Theo sitting on the stump beside his, watching him intently.

Wrapping herself in a cloak, Mercy made her way over to them. As she neared him, Ben quit talking and turned to her, wiping tears from his cheeks. Rolling a stump over, Mercy took a seat on his other side.

"Turns out he's a pretty good listener," Ben said with a sniffle.

"Yes, he is," Mercy agreed. "He's seen my tears plenty of times."

"I tried sleeping," Ben began. "But I can't get their faces out of my head. That boy you had Henry and I carry out of the tent, one of the ones you couldn't save, he was one of my friends."

"I'm sorry, I—"

"He was only sixteen. He'd run away from home after his father was killed in the war last year and joined the militia. I don't even know his last name; I have no way to find his mama and tell her what's become of him."

"Oh, Ben . . ."

"It was horrible, Mercy. The sounds of anguish, like nothing you've ever heard. The Iroquois moved all around us, through us, whooping and screaming. Their faces painted black and red; they danced in the smoke of our muskets. Men would shoot at a warrior standing right in front of them, and after the smoke would clear, there was no one there. . . . We were massacred."

"But you were brave, you made it home."

"I wet myself, Mercy. I was so scared."

"Many men did," Mercy replied. "I've changed plenty of breeches since the engagement."

He shifted his feet in the dirt, looking into the fire. "Thank you," Ben said, kicking a small twig with his toe. "I didn't know that."

"You're still just a boy, Ben . . . and a man. I don't know, you're somewhere in–between. Boys aren't supposed to die at sixteen or be at war. You're supposed to be apprenticing somewhere, learning a trade, planting seed, working for the smith, or learning to run the tavern. Not this . . ."

Benjamin nodded his head.

"You're doing as well, if not better, than many men much older than you. Having endured all that you have, and not running away.... That's incredible, Ben. Adelaide is proud of you, and she ought to be. I'm proud of you too."

He looked at her, a soft appreciative smile on his face. "You're not sore about us?"

"Not at all," Mercy said. "You make a smart match; if anything, I'm jealous."

"Why? You've got Theo," Ben teased.

"Yes, my soulmate . . ." Mercy said, rolling her eyes and placing her hand on her heart.

Theo looked at both of them, ruffling his feathers.

In the days that followed, General Herkimer died while getting his leg amputated due to infection. There was little time to mourn however, as British General Burgoyne sent the Hessian Colonel Baum, along with the local Loyalist militia, to Bennington, Vermont, to steal and destroy Continental supplies while his main army continued to push south, engaging General Gates near Saratoga.

Benjamin and Henry's riflemen were again called upon to support General Stark at Bennington while Mercy, Adelaide, and

Abigail stayed and cared for Gates' wounded men. Fortunately for the Continentals, it had rained the entire day on the 15th, slowing the redcoats' progress as they marched along muddy roads towards New York, and allowing the Patriots to catch their breath.

Before the battle of Bennington, General Stark gathered his men and told them defeat was not an option. He said either he'd win, or his wife would go to sleep that night a widow. During a long week locked in battle, General Stark sent the local militia to the Hessian General Baum disguised as Loyalists. The fighting turned to hand–to–hand combat atop a muddy hill, but eventually, due to Stark's ruse, the Patriots were able to surround Baum, and the victory was won, saving the precious Continental supplies.

In the face of the defeat at Bennington, General Burgoyne, having lost many soldiers, was forced to withdraw. Many of the Loyalists, including local native allies, abandoned the British mission, feeling mislead and sorely used. As awful as the fighting had been, it was a major Continental victory.

Henry and Benjamin had marched home with their unit, leaving the local militia to secure Bennington against further attack. They'd arrived exhausted, covered in drying mud from head to toe, not a man amongst them without a scratch. There was no time for hot baths, the soldiers were marched to the stream to bathe while the women washed and mended their clothes.

Mercy and Adelaide took turns boiling rags and cleaning and bandaging wounds. Many a man stared up at them with hollow eyes, still in shock at having fought so many of their friends and neighbors. A victory of that kind has little to rejoice about.

More of Benjamin and Adelaide's time spent together was in comforting silence rather than talk, neither of them able to communicate the things they'd seen and endured.

Theo, however, was a welcome distraction as he playfully demanded Mercy's attention. For the first time in weeks, the four Youngs and Adelaide wandered the camp looking for critters for the owl to hunt. Everywhere they went, Theo brought smiles to weary soldiers' faces who were eager to point the way to the last place they'd seen a pesky rodent or a fluffy squirrel.

After an hour or two, Theo had caught three mice and a very portly rat to the praise and adulation of everyone standing by. On their way back to the wagon, at the edge of camp, Benjamin spotted a rabbit near the edge of the clearing, roughly fifty yards away. The band froze in their tracks, and Mercy twisted her body so Theo was pointed towards their quarry.

The rabbit hopped once in the shaggy grasses and Theo's head snapped to attention, his eyes growing wide.

"That's it," Mercy said under her breath. "Rabbit stew would taste divine tonight."

Theo's talons began kneading her shoulder pad in anticipation of her command.

"Alright, boy," she whispered. "Hunt!"

Theo leapt from her shoulder, banking hard while climbing higher and higher in the sky. Circling the rabbit at high altitude, he determined its blind side before folding his wings and dropping towards the creature at incredible speed.

Just as it appeared Theo would crash into the ground, he spread his wings, swinging himself upward, while at the same time slamming his talons into the shocked rodent with devastating force, dragging it several feet before coming to a halt.

"He did it!" Abe exclaimed.

The younger boys darted across the open ground, racing to be the first to reach him.

"He makes it look so easy," Adelaide said.

"He's as effective as a rifle," Ben agreed.

Reaching Theo, Mercy held out one of the mice he'd already caught in exchange for the rabbit. Theo climbed off, and David lifted it proudly.

"Mama's gonna be happy to see this," David said.

On their way back to the wagon, they passed a trio of bandaged soldiers looking haggard and forlorn. They sat heavily around a small smoldering fire, attempting to keep the swarms of mosquitos at bay. David stopped suddenly, looking at the rabbit, then back to the soldiers. Without asking permission, he turned and walked the rabbit over to them.

One of the men, with a bandage over his eye, smiled warmly at David as he handed him the rabbit, ruffling his hair in playful appreciation. The other two men nodded their heads, thanking him for the kind gesture. Then David turned and walked back to his siblings.

"That's just what Papa would've done," Benjamin said, putting his arm around his little brother.

They made their way back to the wagon, less one rabbit, but feeling fuller than they had in a while. Mercy was proud of him, he had the heart to see his own need, yet recognize someone whose need was greater, and the strength to choose sacrifice instead.

They reached their wagon just as light rain began to fall, making it an even dozen storms in the last two weeks. The rivers were swollen, the fields saturated, the roads a maze of ruts and puddles, a march to anywhere would be miserable. It was becoming an all–consuming effort simply to keep food and supplies from rotting.

Thankfully, their wagon canvas was well sealed, keeping their humble home warm and dry. Just being up off the ground was a blessing few shared, and Mercy found the comforting patter of rain lulled her to sleep far better than an eerie silence. At least here the redcoats were suffering as much as they were, unlike those under General Howe quartered in New York. Here the weather would be dampening spirits on both sides.

Chapter 13

On August 25th, Mercy learned that Continental General Benedict Arnold had arrived at Fort Stanwix and broke the British siege. The fort was now safe, along with the Mohawk Valley, and with Arnold's troops supporting General Gates, General Burgoyne had his hands full.

British General Howe, seeing his countrymen had been stalled in the north, finally made his move. Using an armada of 265 ships, Howe landed seventeen thousand redcoats at Head of Elk, Maryland, in preparation for a march on the American capital, Philadelphia.

With this new threat in the south, Lt. Davis and his staff were called back to support General Washington, while Henry and Ben were ordered to continue supporting Gates. For the first time, the family would be divided; Henry and Ben fighting on the northern front, and the girls serving on the southern. The road back to New York had been a somber one.

On the way, they were informed that their journey would take an added day, as General Washington had decided to move his army south to Wilmington, Delaware, to cut off General Howe from marching north to capture Philadelphia. It was a race.

As the wagon shook and teetered down the sloppy road, Mercy could feel the ache in Abigail and Adelaide's hearts. Ben and Henry had been gone plenty of times on missions, sometimes deep into British territory, but this was different. There was no guarantee they would ever see each other again.

The Continentals were trapped between General Burgoyne in the north, Howe in the South, and the British Navy to the East. To the west was wild uncharted territory, Native country, lands not yet open to the colonials. They were running out of room to retreat.

"How come we keep running away?" David asked as they started the third day of their journey. "How can we win if we don't just fight them?"

"Because wars are not decided by battles, but money," Lt. Davis answered. "For the British the war is much more costly; their troops and supplies have to be shipped to the colonies. Support of that kind is very expensive. The Continentals, on the other hand, are supplied here in the colonies. Our troops are recruited locally, and many of them are fighting with little or no pay. Our supplies, too, are grown and raised right here, making the war much less expensive for us. Therefore, the king needs to end the war as swiftly as possible in order to win. But the Continentals don't need to win a single battle, only outlast the king's resources in order to win."

"You're saying the redcoats are better at war than us?" David asked.

"Yes, in almost every way," Lt. Davis answered. "But time is their greatest enemy. And what we lack in experience, we more than make up for in grit and determination. Washington isn't trying to beat them; he's going to let them beat themselves."

"Runnin' away is an awful lot of work," David complained.

"Aye, it is," Lt. Davis agreed.

"Especially with this endless rain," Abigail said. "Poor boys out there are marching in mud up to their breeches."

"Our scouts have reported the Brits are faring no better," Lt. Davis replied. "The weather will test both armies, and we must pray we prove to have the greater endurance."

When they arrived in Wilmington, Lt. Davis was ordered not to unpack. The army needed to be ready to move at a moment's notice, care of casualties would have to take place in makeshift covered wagons. The battle was going to be a moving battle, one where a moment of hesitation could spell disaster.

Howe would make a move, and Washington would have to counter that move. Spies, lookouts, and runners would be of utmost importance. Dispatch riders would have to ride long distances through hostile country to deliver messages between the two fronts, coordinating their efforts to keep the colonies out of the king's hand. Because of this, the king put a high price on capturing the riders before their messages could be delivered. Only the most cunning would survive his gauntlet.

This season of fighting was to be the greatest test the Americans had yet to face. A loss would mean the war was over. A victory only meant it would continue, the hardships would continue, and America would continue. Their tired bodies and souls would choose the former, but their spirits could only accept the latter.

Spies relayed information that Howe had planned on moving towards Philadelphia as soon as the army had landed, but the rain had spoiled so much powder and supplies that he'd been forced to wait for more to arrive. Washington too had suffered the same misfortune as he'd raced to Wilmington to intercept and was himself, in the hunt for fresh munitions. The weather currently had the two armies at a standstill.

It wasn't until August 30th that the redcoats and Continentals finally met in battle. Washington had wisely secured two hills, Iron Hill and Grey's Hill, overlooking the British route. When Mercy awoke that morning, the clouds had finally parted, and the sun shone brightly on the beginnings of a beautiful and fateful day. She chose to ignore the smells of drying mud and worms as she stepped her way carefully along the board path laid across the yard between the supply wagons and the medical wagons.

Her dresses had a permanent dingy stain about the hem, and she hardly made an effort to lift it anymore. Most of her current patients suffered from foot rot, or scabies, a nasty parasite that burrowed under the skin, due to the foul damp living conditions, and general lack of hygiene.

She found Lt. Davis sitting near a small fire smoking a pipe while he waited for his kettle to boil. The sun seemed to have him in higher spirits, and he apparently felt no need to rush from its warmth; his patients wouldn't be going anywhere.

"Good morning, Mercy," he said as she approached.

"Good morning, sir," she answered.

"Will Adelaide be joining you?" he asked.

"She will, the post rider just arrived and she's franticly penning Benjamin a letter before he goes. I told her you would understand."

"I feel no need to rush things on such a glorious day," he said. "I finished treatment of most of our patients before dawn, but when I saw its glow on the canvas, I couldn't allow myself to forgo the comforts of its rays; not after so many a dreary day. Washington himself rode to the top of Iron Hill yonder to look upon the enemy in the fair light."

No sooner had the words escaped his mouth, than the rumblings of cannons echoed across the valley. Moments later, plumes of smoke rose from the hilltop as the guns on Iron Hill returned fire.

Instantly the hastily constructed camp was a frenzy as soldiers and civilians ran to their positions.

"Blast!" Lt. Davis fumed. "It was going to be such a fine day."

A soldier ran up, saluting Lt. Davis. "I've been ordered to tell you to have your people ready to move. It's General Cornwallis and the Hessians, we won't be able to hold the hill. Be prepared to retreat with the supplies."

"Understood," Lt. Davis said.

"I'll spread the word." Mercy curtsied.

Lt. Davis nodded, dashing off to alert the rest of his staff, while Mercy went to collect Abigail, Abe, and David, hoping Adelaide was still at the wagon.

British cannons continued softening the hilltop for the better part of an hour, before they were replaced by the sharp sound of musket fire as the regulars and Hessians began their assault. The Continental militia holding the hill returned fire in sporadic succession.

Abigail and the boys packed up their wagon, while Adelaide and Mercy helped Lt. Davis. All around them blocks of soldiers either moved towards the enemy or away, as General Washington moved to counter Cornwallis by securing a new position.

The supply train, and most of the medical staff, including Abigail and the boys, retreated to the Brandywine River, where Washington planned to set up his new defensive position. Mercy, Adelaide, and Lt. Davis stood by to assist in the evacuation of any wounded from the battle. Above them, the fighting on the hill grew desperate, and she could already see men retreating down the backside of the hill.

"Best be ready," Lt. Davis said. "The redcoats will be on their heels."

The rest of the militia retreated haphazardly down the hill, firing as they went.

"Get out of here, doctor!" an officer said, riding up to them. "The hill is lost, and you'll be in range when they get their big guns in place! Go, we'll bring the wounded to you at Brandywine!"

Lt. Davis took one last look at the hill before cracking the reigns. They both knew that many of the wounded would be left on the hill, under the care of British surgeons, whose duty it was to put the king's men first.

Arriving at the Brandywine river, fighting positions were already under construction. Lt. Davis parked their covered flatbed just as more clouds began to roll in. In less than an hour the rain was falling steadily once more. Fortunately for Washington, Cornwallis was satisfied with taking Iron Hill, and given the rain and risk of losing more powder, had decided to call it a day, giving the Americans precious time to prepare.

Chapter 14

September 1, 1777

Today General Washington read to us glad tidings from General Gates. The redcoats near Saratoga, under General Burgoyne, have been repulsed yet again as they were attempting to push further south. Our northern front is holding, preventing the British from encircling Washington, and ending the war.

We've had no word from Benjamin and Henry, correspondence has been limited for a time so that information is not inadvertently given to the enemy. I trust that they are well and fighting proudly as I've only known them to do. Their special unit is sure to be engaged regularly as it is the will of General Washington that the redcoats are constantly pestered.

Benjamin turns seventeen today, he's all but buried the boy he was when we left Lexington. I wish he were here to celebrate with. On this day I'm reminded to thank the Lord for the blessing of his birth; a girl never had a better older brother. I pray by the grace of God he will be spared to celebrate his next birthday together a year from now.

Abigail and I have also been rather engaged as of late. No sooner had we arrived in Brandywine than David and Abe set out to collect firewood for the fires. They've become so proficient at the task that they have oft received commendation for their work. This time, however, Abigail and I were still in the process of sorting the wagon from our journey when we heard the two of them crying out and hollering somewhere down by the river.

Abigail dropped the kettle she'd been carrying right where she stood and set off after them. She's gotten awful lean and quick since moving into camp last spring. When we reached the boys, I'd first thought they'd killed a beaver, as a large rodent–like creature lay in the leaf litter near them, but upon closer inspection I recognized it as a porcupine.

Both of the boys were covered in stickers up and down their legs, and Abe had somehow managed to get a few in his arm. Abigail scooped David up as best she could, being careful of the stickers, and made for Lt. Davis. I did my best to help Abe, but his condition was so miserable he had to limp himself on both legs to the doctor. Abe's ability to hold his pain could rival that of any man I've ever known.

Abigail nearly cried as Lt. Davis and I cut away the boy's breeches, their peppered legs had already begun to swell. It turns out, David had been collecting branches near some young pine shoots unaware the critter had already claimed that spot. By the time he recognized his mistake, the rodent had already taken a swing.

Abe had been collecting branches a little ways away and when David yelped in pain, he'd charged in to save him unaware of what it was that had attacked him. By the time Abe realized his mistake, the porcupine had taken a swing at him as well. This would have been the end of it, but Abraham, occasionally bad tempered, took a swing at the creature out of offense. His branch struck the critter, killing it, but not before it put a few quills in Abe's arm.

Lt. Davis removed eighty quills from David, and over one hundred from Abe. Abe held his own, biting down on a leather roll, but David was beside himself, especially when the turpentine was added to the wounds to prevent infection. Abigail, bless her soul, was wet with tears by the end of the ordeal. Before today, I'd never laid eyes on a porcupine, and after today, I'm satisfied that I have seen enough.

The boys will be laid up for a spell, and their dressings will need to be changed regularly. Abigail is worried, infection has taken more souls than the redcoats. Abe is indignant and swears to rid the world of porcupines just as soon as he is able. David, on the other hand, seems to be enjoying all Abigail's fussing over him, I fear he aims to delay his recovery as long as possible. Still, his whimpers as I lay writing break my heart, and I'm beginning to understand how a boy could have so many stories as Mr. Hadley. It is an act of God that any of them survive to be men.

Mercy Young, 14 years old

"Any idea where so many of the militia are off to today?" Mercy asked Lt. Davis as he checked the boys' wounds.

"General Washington has sent them into the countryside between here and the enemy to remove any livestock and food stores that may be captured as the redcoats advance," Lt. Davis replied. "He's even ordered the millstones removed from the mills and carried away, so they're unable to grind their own flour."

"I thought the redcoats were supplied by sea?" Abe winced as Lt. Davis prodded his leg.

"They are, but the further they move inland, the harder it is to transport supplies from the coast and the more susceptible they are to raids. It takes a considerable amount of food to sustain such a large force, it is much more prudent to supply it locally than to remain dependent on deliveries from the coast. The more we can hamper their efforts of local supply, the more effort they must invest in survival rather than fighting."

"Many of the local folks are not going to like the fact their goods are being taken by the Continentals," Mercy said.

"I fear they would be taken at any rate," Lt. Davis replied. "An unfortunate consequence of war."

"Hopefully they can understand it," Mercy replied. "Henry said that if we lose the affections of Americans, we are no better than the king."

"Well, boys," Lt. Davis said. "I see no signs of infection yet, but we must keep these wounds clean. Abigail and Mercy will scrub them twice a day with soap. After that, more turpentine until the wounds are closed."

"Not turpentine," David moaned. "It burns!"

"If you'd like, I could remove your leg," Lt. Davis replied dryly.

David's eyes went wide. "No! The turpentine is fine!"

"That's a good lad," Lt. Davis said, ruffling his hair. "Now, I must see to my other patients. No getting up and about, not for a couple more days. With all this mud and filth, it could be the death of you."

"They'll listen," Abigail assured him.

Lt. Davis packed his things and started for the medical wagons, with Adelaide on his heels. Mercy gave each of the boys an encouraging squeeze of the hand before collecting Theo and following after them.

"Being cooped up in that wagon is likely to be more painful than the quills," Mercy said, catching up to them.

"As a young boy, I'd have felt the same," Lt. Davis replied.

"Have you ever dealt with porcupine quills before?" Adelaide asked.

"My father has, I seem to recall one of our neighbors had a dog that got tangled up with one. Had quills all about its muzzle. My father removed them, and the dog lived for many years after, though I believe it'd lost an eye."

"Poor thing," Mercy said.

"If I remember right, the ol' boy was pampered much like your bird. I don't think he regretted his life."

When they reached the medical wagons, Lt. Davis stopped them for a moment. "I must tell you ladies; we've been given strict orders concerning the coming battles. We do not have the numbers necessary to beat the enemy in open war, but if you remember, our aim is to have them beat themselves. As such, when the British advance upon us, we are only to tend to those who are likely to be able to return to the fight. The rest we are to leave to the British surgeons. Collecting and caring for our wounded will further slow their progress and drain their resources," Lt. Davis said.

"That's awful," Adelaide said. "You know they will only receive care after the redcoats have helped themselves. Many of them will die before they're seen."

"Those are *our* men, Americans, we can't just leave them out there," Mercy agreed.

"Those are our orders," Lt. Davis said. "The redcoats are better supplied than we are. Even if we wanted to, a quick retreat is no time to pick up the wounded. By leaving them to the British, they will still be of service. I don't like it any better than you do, but their sacrifices will all be for nothing if our cause should fail. We must make full use of every advantage, even ones as dire as these."

Adelaide looked at Mercy in sorrowful disbelief. Now, even the wounded were reduced to obstacles on the battlefield. Mercy knew Lt. Davis was as troubled as they, but he was a soldier, and couldn't afford to let it show. She prayed in advance for the boys they'd leave behind to the loneliness of mud, blood, and smoke.

Mercy went about her work in a fog, the lines of morality and nobleness of the cause no longer as black and white as she'd believed them to be. She couldn't help but wonder if the same orders had been given to General Gates, and should something happen to her brother or Henry, would they just be left in the mud to slow the enemy?"

"You must be disappointed in me," Lt. Davis said as he watched her.

She looked up at him, her mind returning to the moment. "You're a soldier," Mercy replied. "It can't be helped."

"Still," he said, "my conscience plagues me with the cruelty of it. Men who deserve honor for their sacrifice, being left behind because they can no longer stand on the very field they suffered great injury defending."

"What cause is worth such suffering? Does the general not see the unrighteousness of it?" Mercy asked.

"General Washington can't afford to look at things the way we do. His is to choose between the cruelest of fates and suffer the derision of his countrymen for whatever he should choose. If we are to win, there are no right choices, only to endure, and pray our consciences will one day forgive us."

That night a chaplain who traveled with the army named Reverend Joab Trout prayed with the Continentals and militia who would soon face the enemy.

"Soldiers and countrymen, we have met this evening perhaps for the last time. We have shared the toil of the march, the peril of the fight, and the dismay of the retreat alike; we have endured the cold and hunger, and the contumely of the infernal foe. And we have met in the peaceful valley. We have gathered together— God grant it may not be for the last time. It is a solemn moment. Under the shadow of a pretext, under the sanctity of the name of God, invoking the Redeemer to their aid, do these foreign hirelings lay our people. They may conquer us tomorrow. Might and wrong may prevail and we may be driven from the field— but the hour of God's own vengeance will come. How dread the punishment. The eternal God fights for you and will triumph. God rest the souls of the fallen. When we meet again, may the shadow of twilight be flung over a peaceful land. God in Heaven grant it."

Chapter 15

It was around nine o'clock in the morning on September 3rd, while in the middle of changing the boys' dressings, that Mercy heard the first shots. The shooting was sporadic at first, the sharp cracking sound of rifles. It was General Washington's newly formed sharpshooter corps under General Maxwell, engaging the British at Cooch's Bridge, a crossing over a small creek only a mile or so away.

Presently, there was a uniform racket of dull musket fire, the regulars had returned fire. This was followed by more rifle fire, and then musket fire again. The boys looked at each other nervously as she finished wrapping their bandages.

"They're coming, Mercy," David said.

"Don't worry," Mercy replied. "We'll be ordered to move out with the supplies long before they get here. The sharpshooters are only slowing them down a bit."

"I know Henry said runnin' away was part of the plan, but it sure would be nice to lick them once in a while," Abe replied.

"You boys look to be healing up well," Mercy said. "I didn't see any infection and your wounds are nearly closed."

"Still awful tender," Abe confessed.

"Yeah," David groaned.

"Well, they went pretty deep," Mercy sighed.

"Noah shoulda thrown them critters out of the ark," David said.

"Skunks too," Abe agreed.

"I'm sure they must have some purpose," Mercy said. "God wouldn't have made them otherwise."

"Maybe He stepped away from the workbench for a minute and one of the angels gave it a try," Abe said. "That'd make a whole lot more sense. I've made all kinds of abominations when Henry's left the tools out—at least that's what Abigail called 'em."

Even Mercy had to smile at that notion. "Well, you boys rest easy. Abigail will be by in a bit. I need to be off in case Lt. Davis gets ordered to run a wagon to the sharpshooters," Mercy said.

"Why can't Adelaide do that?" Abe asked.

Mercy stopped. "Because—because I'm the one who goes with him, that's why," she said, jumping out of their wagon.

Arriving near the medical wagons, she found Lt. Davis harnessing up a flatbed.

"Do we have orders to go fetch them?" Mercy asked.

"Not yet, but it's better to be prepared," Lt. Davis said. "How are the boys?"

"Better, no infection. Abe is a little salty it's taking so long to heal; he's beginning to question your practices," Mercy said.

"Well, it was my first time, and there's nothing in the books. He may be right."

"Don't tell him that," Mercy said. "He'll somehow manage to spread it to the whole camp that you don't know what you're doing."

"Will the redcoats make it this far today?" Adelaide asked as she returned from one of the medical wagons.

"The scouts say it's an advance party, Hessians again. Several hundred of them, but Maxwell is making them pay for every step. General Maxwell has his men fighting like the natives, hiding behind the trees, firing and then moving before the redcoats can return fire. I've been told they're sustaining very few, if any, casualties thus far," Lt. Davis said.

"Maybe someone told 'em they'd be left behind if they did," Adelaide said in contemp.

"We'd best get the rest of the wagons ready to travel just in case," Lt. Davis replied, choosing to ignore her comment.

The riflemen resisted continuously as the British pushed towards the bridge, but Lt. Davis was ordered to hold. The horses pawed the ground, even they seemed to be anxious to perform their duty, but still they waited. At long last the rate of shooting began to die down, a rider confirmed that the sharpshooters had shot themselves out of ammunition and seeing they were no match for British bayonets, were preparing to fall back.

The order was given, and the marksmen made a hasty retreat back towards the Brandywine. As they came into view, Lt. Davis drove the flatbed out to meet them. Fortunately, only a handful amongst them needed care, though it was reported that several dead and mortally wounded were left behind in the care of the Hessians.

Lt. Davis loaded three men who'd been slashed by British bayonets onto the flatbed and drove them back to camp while Mercy began preliminary treatment.

"We gave it to 'em good," one of the soldiers said. He had a long gash across his thigh, but fortunately it hadn't reached the artery.

"We coulda done better," another man said, "if not for our miserable lieutenants."

"They're unseasoned is all," the first man said.

"It's getting towards evening," the third man said. "They'll hang it up for today. The redcoats didn't get far."

"They won't delay long," the first man said as Lt. Davis pulled the wagon to a halt. "Winter will be here soon."

"That they won't," Lt. Davis agreed, slipping into the back to help Mercy.

"That owl always follow you around?" the second soldier asked. "I can't tell if it's lookin' at me . . ." He swallowed hard. ". . . Or through me."

"Oh, that's just Theo. My very first patient," Mercy said. "He took a liking to me and—"

"Now they're inseparable." Lt. Davis frowned.

"Ah, well, he's a might observant, isn't he," the man said.

"I think he thinks he's lookin' out for me," Mercy said.

"Well, it's working," the man replied.

After the men were patched up, Lt. Davis gave them stern instructions to watch for infection and turned them loose. It was better they were back with their units than left behind. Mercy watched them go, making their way over to the fires flickering brightly in the dusky light.

Theo ruffled his feathers on her shoulder. It would be night soon, and he'd disappear for a time, but he was always back by morning. She missed their walks in the woods, the trapping and fishing, adventures with Mr. Hadley. . . . The war moved so fast now, and her job as a nurse was indispensable. Everything was changing, they *all* were changing.

She walked back to their wagon with Adelaide by the light of the sentry fires. Their patients being so few, Abigail elected to stay with the boys and Mrs. Bell all day and baby them. In truth, it was probably the only way to keep Abraham from wandering off. It was always eerie, going to bed with the redcoats only a few miles away. They could be roused at any moment amongst a great commotion of being set upon by the enemy and be forced to evacuate with all haste.

All they could do was wait and pray.

On September 8th, Mercy woke to the banging of drums and a bugle's song. Fear washed over the wagon as everyone fought to find their garments in the dark. The night was black as could be, Abe checked a pocket watch by firelight, revealing it to be only 3 a.m. Everywhere folks and soldiers ran in a frenzy, but Mercy knew the fastest way to get information would be to find Lt. Davis.

Giving Abigail a quick peck on the cheek, Mercy jumped from the wagon. "Don't worry, Mama," she called. "I'll find out what's going on and be right back."

"Mercy!" Abigail called, but it was too late.

Mercy dashed across the field towards the medical wagons, hardly bothering to lift her hem. When she reached the wagons, she found Lt. Davis already busily harnessing the teams.

"What is it?" Mercy huffed, stopping beside him.

"Howe has deployed the Hessians; they're heading this way."

"How soon?" Mercy asked.

"I haven't been told," he replied, buckling a strap. "Not for an hour I suspect. Is your family in order?"

"We're working on it, it's slower with the boys injured. Mama's gonna need my help. I'll be back as soon as I can." And she set off into the dark once more.

When she arrived back at their wagon, Abe was hobbling about helping Abigail and Mrs. Bell harness their horses.

"What did you hear?" Abigail asked.

"General Howe's Hessians are on their way, marching as we speak. Lt. Davis said they could arrive within the hour."

"Have we been ordered to relocate?" Mrs. Bell asked.

"Not yet, just to be ready," Mercy said.

"We will be," Abe said confidently.

Agonizing hours passed without so much as a shot. The Hessians were indeed on the move, but to where? Continentals and militia alike, shifted uneasily in their fighting positions and trenches along the river. If the waiting was a part of the British strategy, it was working. The silence of ten thousand straining ears was like the powder in a musket. A single spark, and the silence would transform into the deafening din of war.

Finally, at 9 a.m. the Hessians arrived at the Brandywine and the fighting commenced. The Hessians and militia made a direct assault on the Continental lines, smoke from muskets and cannons blurred Mercy's vision. Lt. Davis squinted into the haze beside her, ready to send the team into the fray at a moment's notice.

The Hessians were fierce, they fought differently than the regulars, their resolve was difficult to break. The Continentals would push them back, only to have them reform and come at them again. The Patriots held the high ground, and having had time to dig proper trenches, casualties were few, but there was a problem.

After several hours of fighting, it was apparent this was not the full measure of Howe's army. A large portion, consisting mostly of British regulars, was missing from the fight. General Washington sent out scouts, and that's when the Continentals figured out Howe's real plan.

The Hessians had only been a diversion, sowing their lives dearly, so Howe could lead his army around Iron Hill and flank General Washington's army. By the time Howe's movements were discovered, General Washington only had moments to send troops to support his flank before an entire collapse of the army took place, and they were surrounded.

Soldiers moved in a panic, now their limited numbers had to fight on two fronts. Washington called an emergency meeting of his generals to determine what to do. They couldn't go forward or backward, and the British Navy cut off their escape by sea. Howe had outsmarted him.

Chapter 16

By nightfall the British had hemmed the Continentals in. The situation was beyond desperate, the cause dangled by a thread. Howe, seeing that the Patriots were without escape and that his men could use a rest, decided to call it a day and make camp. He'd finish off General Washington in the morning.

Mercy, Adelaide, and Lt. Davis worked feverishly to treat as many soldiers as they could and get them back out onto the line. Everyone knew the Hessians had not forgotten the battle of Trenton, the American attack on Christmas night. Their enemies would not be wrong for returning the insult now.

Many shadows swayed and bobbed in the glow of Washington's tent. His generals desperately looked for a solution that didn't end in surrender.

Some of the soldiers Mercy worked on grumbled about Washington's ineptitude as commander and chief, citing their many losses, and how often the British generals got the upper hand. Lt. Davis said their sentiments were shared by many, and that Washington's position was indeed in jeopardy, as was the cause, though it mattered little in their current circumstances.

Mercy prayed as she worked. The British command had done well, but their cause could not end here, not yet. She prayed that the Lord would show the generals a way.

At midnight orders were passed via whisper, the Continentals would quietly pack up, stoke the fires so they burned bright, leave the tents in place, and attempt to sneak away into Pennsylvania under the cover of darkness. It was a risky maneuver, if they were caught on the road, strung out in long columns with no protection, they, and the cause, would be destroyed.

Again, horse's hooves would have to be wrapped, and wagon wheels covered with fabric. Anything that clattered or rattled was wrapped or tightened. Their banners were cloaked, and everything that shined was darkened with soot.

By 2 a.m. the march was underway. Quietly they escaped, right through a gap in the enemy lines, an entire army, making nary a sound. Washington continued long into the morning until they happened upon a favorable spot further up the Brandywine outside of Howe's trap. It was a miraculous march. If General Howe was a master of battle, Washington was a master of retreat.

By dawn's light, the haggard Continentals began digging trenches along a six–mile stretch of the Brandywine, knowing the British, after a full night's rest, would be at them in the morning.

Mercy's eyes burned and her hands ached as she, Adelaide, and Lt. Davis helped weary soldiers dig trenches.

They were nearly done with the first trench when she realized Theo was missing. He'd left for his nightly rounds before their march and hadn't returned by the time they'd left. Panic seized her, what if he came back to find them and the redcoats did something to him? What if he'd thought she'd left him behind on purpose and never returned? What if he was killed?

She looked back the way they'd come. She wanted to call out to him, but they were under strict orders. Surely the redcoats would move in and occupy their old position in the morning, and if he were there, surely they would find it odd and dispatch him. Immediately, she began to pray, this time for her dear friend, for his safety, that by God's shepherding hand he would find his way home.

Mercy woke later that morning. She'd fallen asleep for a couple hours in spite of her fears for Theo. She felt ragged, worn to the bone, and though she usually passed when offered coffee, today would be different. Glancing hopefully out at the backboard, her heart sank, Theo had not returned. A sickening dread filled her famished stomach.

Looking around the wagon, she was surprised to find that only herself and the boys remained. Adelaide and Abigail were already up and about, or perhaps they hadn't slept at all. Pulling on her dress, she crept out of the wagon.

Outside, she found the camp busy with exhausted soldiers, trying to get a little food and coffee into themselves before the redcoats arrived. Surely by now, Washington's escape had been discovered, and their new whereabouts relayed back to a shocked General Howe.

From near the supply wagons, she saw Abigail and Adelaide heading her way. They were moving fast, and Abigail had a concerned look on her face; well, she always had a concerned look on her face, but this time it was more concerned.

When they reached Mercy, Abigail took her hands. "The redcoats have already been sighted on the road, and General Washington is fixing to make a stand. They're saying this battle could decide the war. . . . Mrs. Bell's husband has ordered her and the children back to Boston to weather the storm, and I—" she looked away. "And I'm going to send the boys with her."

Mercy wrapped her arms around her; their family was being pulled apart.

"We haven't much time," Abigail said, wiping a tear.

"Are you going too?" Mercy asked Adelaide.

"No, Lt. Davis needs all the help he can find, and I'm afraid my mind would wander to dreadful places if I didn't have so much work to do."

Mercy nodded, giving her a hug, and Abigail joined them. "Oh, my precious girls, our suffering is of a different stripe, but it's no less in pain."

"I'll help get the wagon ready," Mercy said.

"And I'll prepare the boys," Abigail agreed.

The wagon was ready in no time, and Abe and David joined Mrs. Bell, Mable, and Nathaniel with little protest. For the second time, Mercy watched her brothers pull away from camp, uncertain of what their world would look like the next time they met. Abigail sent them with a letter for Mr. Hadley explaining the predicament and thanking them for taking in the boys once more, a thing Mercy knew they'd be glad to do.

The three ladies stood holding one another in the bitterness of the moment, wanting nothing more than a minute to cry it out, but knowing they had none.

As the wagon disappeared behind the bend, Abigail gave them a final squeeze. "All right, girls. Let's prepare."

Work continued on Continental fortifications, and General Maxwell's sharpshooters were again sent across the Brandywine to harass the enemy as they approached. The supply train was readied for retreat, and only a couple medical flatbeds would need to be prepared. They'd be leaving most of the wounded behind.

As she worked, Mercy kept one hopeful eye on the sky, willing Theo to find them. Lt. Davis spent the morning combing the trenches treating insignificant wounds that, if infected, could cost a man his life. And everyone waited, worked and waited, waited for the inevitable red serpent to descend on them and begin the fight for their lives again.

All day long riders came and went reporting on the British progress. The British General Howe, was a careful general, rarely did he ever make a move without meticulous reconnaissance. His caution and careful planning had won him so many victories in the past. His strategy was to make it appear he was doing one thing, while secretly doing another, making it incredibly difficult for Washington and his staff to predict what he was actually going to do.

Further word arrived relaying that British General Burgoyne was fixing to march against General Gates in the north. The king was demanding results, and the British generals were fixing to give it to him. From the north and south the redcoats fanned out like two massive hands ready to smash the American rebellion between them.

By day's end, the redcoats had set up camp a short distance from the Brandywine, the ever–careful Howe wanted the day to assess the battlefield and figure out his strategy. Tomorrow they were sure to come. Washington believed that Howe's force, which outnumbered their own by nearly seven thousand, would hit the Continentals head on, relying on superior numbers, equipment, and training to win the day. He'd therefore strengthened the American center in preparation. In the morning they'd know the truth.

For the second night, there was no Theo. The wagon seemed empty without the boys. Again, the cause, her fragile world, hung by a thread. Everyone was exhausted; the redcoats plagued their lives by day, and their minds by night. Her weary hand struggled to pen her hope that felt like madness in her diary. Her weary soul longed for just one peaceful day in the sunlight, playing again as a little girl on the green in Lexington. One day away from this dark, wet, weary place.

Chapter 17

The Battle of Brandywine began on the morning of September 11th, 1777. The Continentals waited wearily in their trenches on their side of the Brandywine as the soft grays of dawn gave way to the rising sun. Lazy smoke drifted up through the green leaves of trees lining the creek. Soft chatter rose from nervous lips as boys and men prepared to meet the enemy once more. Cannons were primed, and their gunners stood ready.

The ladies waited far back from the line with Lt. Davis, watching the road to Chadds Ford. Mercy's heart drummed rapidly in her chest, her instincts priming her for the conflict.

"Remember," Lt. Davis said. "Only those who can return to the battle."

The first shot made her jump; it was somewhat distant, followed by several more. General Maxwell's sharpshooters were engaged. Shot by shot, the crackling of war crept ever closer.

"It's the Hessians," a scout reported. "Coming right at us, there are militia and regulars as well."

General Maxwell's men continued fighting as they retreated towards the ford, slowing the enemy with casualties as they moved to attack the American center. Continental commanders near the trenches encouraged their men to be ready.

Mercy braced herself as the fighting grew close. The clouds of spent powder were now visible and the cracks of muskets sharp and clear. Placing cotton in her ears, she sent up one last prayer for the Lord's salvation of their cause.

Then she could see them, Maxwell's men, racing for the ford. They were narrowly across when the Hessian front came into view, followed by the deafening blasts of Continental cannons. The Hessians poured over the hill like water and rushed towards the ford as the Continentals let loose a volley from the trenches driving them back. The battle had arrived.

Beside her, Abigail prayed aloud as smoke and noise filled the river valley, its peaceful tranquility violated forever. Men cried out on either side, but the battle was too hot for them to rush in. The cannons thundered again, filling the air with smoke that burned her eyes and throat.

The Continentals continued to hold as wave after wave of Hessians and regulars made for the ford only to be driven back by unrelenting fire. Mercy felt as though she were living inside a thunderhead as flashes of light preceded claps of thunder within the swirling smoke.

It went on for hours, neither side willing to yield. Here and there a wounded man would crawl from the cloud and Lt. Davis and Mercy would race to collect them, while Abigail and Adelaide attended to those they'd already retrieved. Stray musket balls riddled the field around them, as panic–stricken men fired their muskets blindly into the smoke.

Soon, British cannons reached the crest of the hills across the river and the Continentals were forced to hunker low in their trenches, allowing the Hessians and regulars to advance. Reinforcements were drawn from the American flanks to help support the center as the British continued their push.

"We're holding them," Lt. Davis said, raising his fist, as another wave of redcoats was forced to retreat.

"The boys are fighting right proudly," Mercy agreed.

Mercy could just make out their banner near the river, its bright stripes and stars standing defiantly in the haze.

The Continentals had fought long into the afternoon when the Hessians finally pulled back to regroup, creating a temporary lull. Mercy and Adelaide raced to the lines with canteens and buckets of water for the soldiers to drink. All around them supply officers replenished ammunition, men ate firecakes savagely from their knapsacks, while others fumbled to light pipes with trembling fingers.

They all looked as though they'd aged a hundred years, their faces and uniforms filthy from lying in the trenches. She wished Theo were there like he'd been on Dorchester Heights. Anything to lift their poor spirits. The men drank all their water with ravenous thirst, causing Mercy and Adelaide to make several trips.

As they made their way back to the water wagon for the third time, Mercy overheard an officer report that General Howe had been sighted racing towards their flank from the north. During the night, he'd marched his regulars nine miles north and crossed the Brandywine upstream in the darkness. Over ten thousand regulars were fixing to smash into their depleted right flank.

Not again . . .

"Mercy, Adelaide!" Lt. Davis called. "We must prepare for retreat at once! Abigail is fetching your wagon, help me with these! We're about to be overrun!"

As he spoke, General Nathaniel Greene and his division raced past at the double–quick, making for the right flank.

"General Greene is going to hold the line as long as he can to give the army a chance to escape. I don't know where yet, but the road to Philadelphia is not yet blocked," Lt. Davis said.

While he was still talking, the first shots rang out from their right flank. With Greene's men pulled from the center, the Hessians also pressed their attack.

Mercy wanted to scream. How could this have happened again?! Why couldn't they ever seem to get the upper hand?

Abigail pulled up in their wagon and climbed down. "Are we ready?" she asked.

"Yes," Lt. Davis answered. "We've been ordered to leave everything and everyone we can't carry. We're setting out now."

Abigail and Mercy climbed up into their wagon, while Adelaide rode with Lt. Davis. As the supply train galloped away from the battle, Mercy struggled to control her emotions. Why was God letting this happen to them? Why couldn't they just win? How were they supposed to outlast the British like this?!

"Try not to fret, Mercy," Abigail said, giving the reigns another crack. "We've run away plenty of times before."

Mercy looked up at her. She may not be saying it, but Abigail looked as discouraged as she felt.

"How can we win if General Howe always catches us off guard?!" Mercy fumed.

"I know it's hard, Mercy; the right path often is, and I don't know much about war, but I do know that we can't win if we surrender," Abigail replied.

Just then Mercy felt a weight slam into her shoulder and sharp pain take hold. "OWWW!" she cried, reaching for the pain.

Her fingers brushed over rough toes and hard talons. Turning, she was eye to eye with Theo! Her eyes flashed open as she snatched him from her shoulder, nearly crushing him in an embrace.

"I knew you'd find me," she said, her eyes filling with tears.

"Well, I'll be . . ." Abigail said. "He must've followed the redcoats right to us."

Mercy released him, setting him on the buckboard beside her.

"He didn't do your shoulder any good," Abigail frowned. "We'll have to get it cleaned up as soon as we make camp."

"I don't mind, Abigail." Mercy grimaced. "I'm just thankful he came back."

Theo looked up at her with the eyes of a starving man.

"I'm sorry, boy," Mercy said, stroking his head. "I don't have anything right now."

"How did he ever survive without you?" Abigail chuffed.

The army retreated towards Philadelphia, fighting every step of the way. General Greene's men brought up the rear, shooting as they went, not stopping to pick up their casualties. At last, as darkness fell, the redcoats, who'd been marching and fighting since the wee hours of the morning, gave up pursuit out of exhaustion.

Washington marched the Continentals until they could barely stand to put some distance between the two armies. Finally, they made a hasty camp near Chester. The soldiers were given orders to sleep out under the stars, and to be ready to set out in retreat at 4 a.m.

Mercy's soul ached for them. Long exhausted faces, marching nearly at a run after such a brutal battle, a humiliating retreat. Filthy, starving, nearly hopeless, they lay out on the damp ground, hoping for a few hours of rest before they'd set off again in the darkness. This wasn't a strategic retreat, this was defeat.

"Not everyone's been counted, but first reports are that we lost nearly twelve hundred men, and two of our cannons," Lt. Davis said as they finished bandaging the blistered soles of their last patient.

"And the redcoats?" Mercy asked.

"Lord only knows for sure," Lt. Davis said, wiping his forehead with the back of his hand. "General Maxwell claims we gave as good as we got."

"If we keep marching like this, we'll lose many more on the road. These poor boys need rest," Mercy said.

"I heard the generals talking," Lt. Davis began. "I probably shouldn't say, but they don't know how the cause can survive. Brandywine was our best shot, and Howe defeated us with ease. Now it's just a matter of time before Burgoyne marches through Gates and crushes us entirely."

"Mama says the Lord will make a way," Mercy replied. "We just have to keep faith."

"It wouldn't be His first time," Lt. Davis sighed. "You best be off, there'll be no coffee in the morning."

Mercy gave a slight curtsy and left for their wagon.

Four a.m. found Mercy on the road to Philadelphia once again. Thousands of tired feet trudged behind their wagon; she could hear their labored breathing, coughing, groaning. It was a testament to their resolve that so many didn't just wander off and leave the cause, though a few of them had already. Officers, faring only slightly better than their men, encouraged them to continue on, praising them for the part they'd played in the battle and their smart retreat, promising victory if they just stayed the course.

It was only a couple of hours before Lt. Davis sent a runner to fetch Mercy to the medical flatbed. Soldiers were falling out due to a lack of footwear and needed to have their feet tended to before they were of no use at all.

Mercy was glad she'd had nothing to eat, the sight of gnarled feet first thing in the morning was trouble for her appetite. After washing away the road, she poured whiskey on a man's feet, causing him to writhe a little. Then she wrapped them carefully in linen cloth and cinched it somewhat tight above the ankle.

Theo watched hungrily from the back of the buckboard, and Mercy half expected him to swoop down and take off with one of the man's toes. She wished she had something to give him, but they hadn't stopped to eat properly in more than a day. Everyone was hungry.

As soon as she finished with the first, two more were added to the wagon. It was a helpless feeling. Soon there wouldn't be room, and the first would have to climb off and continue his march or be left behind. It was going to be a long and difficult day.

By noon Mercy had lost count of patients she'd had, more than fifty. Even so, they were quick to thank her, even as they returned to the hazardous muddy road. Lt. Davis was right, for all they lacked, Americans had grit.

Chapter 18

They'd marched until the day's end and set up camp at dusk at Schuylkill Falls. It was an incredible feat, and spies reported that the British believed Washington's army to still be encamped at Chester because no army could march after the day they'd had. But this American army had.

A day later, word of Howe's astonishment reached the Continental camp, while it wasn't a victory, baffling the British commander gave the Continentals who'd made the miraculous march a bit of pride. General Howe would have to come up with yet another plan if he were to defeat this army.

Washington set the army up in a three–mile–long line from White Horse Tavern to Warren Tavern. Here, they could defend both Philadelphia and Reading, a vital supply town. The British would have to move their army, cannon, and supply train before they'd be ready for another engagement. The grueling marches had paid off, buying the Continentals precious time to prepare and rest.

The medical team worked tirelessly to keep as many men on the line as possible. From Reading, supplies flowed into the camp and the soldiers were able to eat once more. But General Washington was losing favor amongst the men, and morale was at its lowest. It had been a season of defeats, poor conditions, little food, and no pay.

Mercy couldn't fault them for losing heart. This challenge was like nothing any of them could have imagined. All the romantic notions of war that had inspired so many to join the cause seemed little more than lies in the face of the hardships they'd endured. Once again, they found themselves immersed in the "times that try men's souls" that Thomas Paine had written about in *The Crisis*, in desperate need of a victory.

Lt. Davis hadn't heard any further word on how General Gates fared near Saratoga, only that British General Burgoyne was preparing for a major offensive soon. Mercy prayed with all her heart for the safety of Benjamin and Henry, along with Jonathan and Mr. Bell who fought with General Greene. Lastly, she prayed for her papa, that he'd survive, that they all would, and the Good Lord would bring them together once more.

"You ladies have done marvelously these past difficult days," Lt. Davis said, drawing her from her prayers.

"As have you," Mercy replied.

"I think I have things well in hand at the moment, why don't the three of you get some rest."

Mercy could have fallen over; just to *hear* the word rest seemed too good to be true.

"If you're sure," Abigail said.

"I am," Lt. Davis insisted, giving them a bow.

The three of them curtsied in return, and Abigail led them back to the wagon.

"What on earth will we do?" Abigail asked. "We haven't had a rest in a month."

"I think I'll write Benjamin a letter . . . I know he can't receive it now, but he could read it later and know my heart during this time. And, if I'm being truthful, it helps to calm *my* nerves as well," Adelaide said.

"That's a grand idea," Abigail agreed. "Perhaps I'll do the same."

"I think I'll take a walk," Mercy said. "See if Theo and I can rustle up something to eat."

"Don't stray," Abigail chided.

"I won't," Mercy said, giving her a peck on the cheek.

Mercy started towards the trees that lined the river, appreciating the weight of her friend on her shoulder. There were so few constants left in her life, the thought of losing Theo had scared her to death. The soul, it seems, in its love of adventure, still needs things that anchor it. Like a ship that loves the high seas yet still rejoices in a harbor.

Mercy realized that the surer and firmer the anchor, the freer she felt to adventure, knowing the anchor would always be there. But when her world became fraught with uncertainty, her love of adventure faltered, and she longed for the safety of the harbor. Her family was her harbor, and her family was spread all over New England. Her ship had sailed into a turbulent sea, and she was frightened.

She walked along the river, wandering down the tangled paths in her mind. Thoughts she hadn't had time to process over the past month demanded sorting. Theo seemed content to ride along; he'd filled himself up on the march as the wagons had stirred up many shrews and fieldmice along the road.

She found a place in the river, not far from the Continental line, where the water poured over a pile of logs that had been swept downstream by the heavy rains creating a small waterfall. She sat on a rounded boulder watching the stream fall over the logs and churn the water below. Here and there fish darted in the current, their bodies flashing light and dark.

She remembered all the times they'd spent fishing as a family, the joy and elation of a good catch, and the constant competition between her brothers. Innocence. They'd all been so innocent. Now she was wiser. Life had taught her hard lessons, but the cost. . . . She wished they could all go back. But she knew God was good, He could heal wounds no matter where they were found. And perhaps their sacrifice now would mean that other girls and boys in the future could stay in that place—innocence.

Then an idea hit her. Standing up, she brushed the leaves and sticks from her dress and set off briskly for the wagon. When she arrived, she climbed inside and began rooting around.

"Good heavens, Mercy, what's gotten into you?" Abigail asked.

"I'm going fishing," Mercy said.

"You are?!" Adelaide asked.

"Yes, do you want to come?"

"I would, I'm afraid my letter's gone flat. I could use something with a little more joy to write about."

"Found it," Mercy said, holding up a small tin of hooks. "I knew the boys would forget this when they left."

"It makes no difference, Mr. Hadley will have plenty for them," Abigail said.

Mercy grabbed a spool of black thread from her sewing kit. "This should do."

"We haven't any corks." Adelaide frowned.

"That's alright," Mercy said. "I can see the fish dancing, hundreds of them, I don't think we'll need them."

"Don't—" Abigail began.

"We know," Mercy cut her off. "We won't go far, Mama."

Together they jumped down from the wagon, and Mercy grabbed the kindling hatchet hanging on the side.

"What's that for?" Adelaide asked.

"There aren't any canes in these parts so we'll have to do the best we can with a couple of saplings," Mercy replied.

When they reached the small waterfall, Mercy stopped. "Here," she said, handing Adelaide the hatchet. "Find us a couple of long straight saplings, and I'll find us some bait."

Mercy found a large log the size of a man covered in moss and fungus where it lay along the bank a short distance from the water. Pulling on it with all her might, she found it wouldn't budge. After some thought, she sat on the uphill side of the log; with her legs bent, she braced her feet against it and pushed with all her might. It took some effort, but eventually the log gave way and rolled over. Hopping up, she scoured the ground. Several plump juicy worms wriggled in the daylight, and she quickly scooped them up before they could find a new hiding place.

To her dismay, she realized that in her excitement, she'd failed to bring a container to put them in. Wincing, she dropped them into her apron pocket.

"Will these do?" Adelaide asked, holding a couple of slightly curved saplings around six feet long.

"Those will do just fine," Mercy said.

Digging the thread out of her other apron pocket, Mercy tied one end to the tip of a sapling and spooled out about ten feet of thread. She cut the line using the sharp head of the hatchet, before tying on a hook. Lastly, she threaded one of the worms onto the hook; she knew Adelaide didn't like that part.

"Here," Mercy said. "I'll get the other one ready. Toss it right out under the waterfall, and be ready, I don't think it'll take long."

Adelaide took the rod, and Mercy set to work repeating the process.

"Got one," Adelaide cried, swinging a handsome rainbow trout onto the shore.

"See," Mercy beamed. "I knew they'd be hungry."

Theo leapt from Mercy's shoulder, but she was able to catch him as he hopped towards the wriggling fish.

"Nooo, you don't," Mercy chided. "You get the little ones."

Seeming to understand, Theo hopped up on a nearby stump from where he could survey the fishing operation. Adelaide unhooked the trout and threaded it onto a long thin stick the way she'd seen Ben do it.

"Still got my worm," Adelaide smiled.

"Get us another. I'll have this one ready in a minute," Mercy said.

As she finished with her rod, Adelaide swung another fish to shore. It was similar in size to the last, and Theo looked up at Mercy with his big yellow pleading eyes.

"Nope, not that one either," Mercy said.

Mercy's first catch was only slightly smaller than Adelaide's, but Theo's dancing excitement broke through her resolve, and she tossed the fish to him.

"He eats better than all of us," Adelaide said.

"I know," Mercy grumbled. "But he's so sweet—I can't help it."

"I doubt King George gets such good treatment." Adelaide smiled.

"Should start calling him King Theo," Mercy laughed, swinging another fish to shore.

"Don't," Adelaide laughed. "Abigail would have a fit."

"She would," Mercy agreed. "But when he was missing, I could tell she was worried too."

"I think we all were," Adelaide said, tossing Theo another small fish.

Theo jumped up and down as he eyed the two fish. He hadn't gotten halfway through picking apart the first one and he already had another. Both girls laughed as he hopped over and picked up the second fish, laying it next to the first.

"You're going to have to carry him for sure after this, I don't think he's gonna be able to fly," Adelaide said.

They'd each landed more than a dozen fish when Mercy noticed they were being watched. Several soldiers, who must've heard their merriment, stood watching them hungrily.

Mercy nodded subtly to Adelaide who stopped chuckling when she saw the soldiers. Adelaide looked back at Mercy with a soft smile; they both knew what to do.

"You can help yourself," Mercy said, nodding to the sticks of fish.

The men looked at each other for a moment before nearly stumbling over one another to get to the stream.

"Thank you kindly," said one of the soldiers, who was wrinkled and had a graying beard.

Mercy thought she saw tears in his eyes as he slid one of the fish off the stick.

"Tell anyone you see, we'll be catching more," Adelaide said as the men started back up the bank.

"That felt . . . really good," Mercy said with a smile.

Adelaide nodded. "We're gonna need a lot more."

Chapter 19

Mercy, Adelaide, and Abigail were roused by a frantic Lt. Davis a little after midnight on September 16th. Apparently, General Howe had decided they'd had enough rest and was on the move, splitting the British army to attack their flanks. Washington had decided it was time the Americans pull a fast one on General Howe and had roused the army to march out and meet the British on the road where they would be thinned out in a long line.

Lt. Davis and his aides were to remain ready with the supply train, as General Howe had proved to be a formidable and cunning adversary, and everyone needed to be prepared to retreat at a moment's notice. As was her way, Mercy stayed with Lt. Davis on the flatbed following the army, ready to race to the battle when needed. Abigail and Adelaide stayed with the supply train to receive the wounded so Mercy and Lt. Davis could return to the fight.

The morning was crisp, and the air had a subtle bite; fall was near. The first few leaves had begun to change from a vibrant green, to a golden yellow. Apples hung ripe on the trees, and berries were plentiful in the forest. Chestnuts rained through the canopy around them, hitting the ground with a dull thud. It was as fine a fall morning as Mercy could remember.

"Do you think we'll surprise them?" Mercy asked as they rode.

"A year ago, I'd have been sure we'd catch them by surprise, but General Howe seems to know our plans before we know them ourselves. I fear his spies are better than ours, as is his cunning. He will not be easily fooled. If Howe gets word we've set out to meet him, it very well may be ourselves who are caught out in the open."

"I liked it better when you were optimistic," Mercy said.

"Me too," he agreed.

"I've heard the men and officers encouraging one another over the past few days. They've not given up on the hope of freedom."

"Aye," Lt. Davis said. "And if, by the Lord's hand, we make it to winter, it will be a grave loss to the king indeed. He'll be forced to expend his resources over long unfruitful months as the cost of his war grows ever higher. Hence the grueling pace the conflict has taken."

"I keep having to remind myself that surviving *is* winning," Mercy said.

"As do I."

"It seems to be the only kind we're good at."

At two o'clock, Lt. Davis was ordered to remain near White Horse Tavern while the army prepared to engage the enemy. Small skirmishes had broken out between the advance guard of both armies, with the Continentals being forced to flee. The Americans set up on the hills above the road, listening to British drums draw ever nearer.

No sooner had they taken position, than a cool wind began shaking the trees. The beautiful blue sky was rapidly being swallowed by a dreary blanket of churning gray clouds. The fine fall morning seemed to lack the resolve of their cause as it gave way to yet another storm. Within minutes, Mercy's dress became pocked by a fine shower. As the mist fell, the battle began.

The hills obscured their view of the battle, but in a short time she could tell it was not going well. The redcoats fired upon the Continentals with discipline; entire blocks of soldiers all firing on command. The Continentals, on the other hand, returned fire sporadically, much less disciplined; men pulling their triggers out of fear and panic, rather than orders.

"We're falling back," Lt. Davis muttered. "Howe has nearly seventeen thousand men at his disposal, and we only eleven thousand. We lost the element of surprise; this maneuver was an error."

As he spoke, to their horror, a regiment of Hessians appeared on their right flank. A bugle sounded, and the Americans fled from their positions into the soaked valley between them. The rain began to fall harder, and Mercy watched in dismay as the Continentals tried to return fire, but their wet muskets and powder failed them.

The Hessians, realizing their own muskets were useless, drew their hunting swords and charged the fleeing Americans who had neither bayonet nor sword. The wind whipped violently, and the skies grew black as night as the flanked Continentals swung their muskets like clubs, trying to defend themselves.

Mercy's dress clung to her body; she held her hand above her eyes in a vain attempt to shield them from the storm. In each lightening flash, she could barely make out the hordes of redcoats pouring over the hills towards the entrapped Americans.

They were about to lose the war.

The storm intensified still further, turning the road into a muddy river, and the valley to slop. Soldiers on both sides fought to keep their footing as their feet sank up to their shins in mud.

The raindrops stung now as they were thrown violently into her face and neck. Lt. Davis tried to protect her, but the rain seemed to be coming from every direction. Here and there, soaked and muddied soldiers streamed past them in utter confusion. There was another bright flash, the thunder cracking so loudly she threw her face into her lap and covered her ears with her hands.

When she looked up through the driving rain, seeing only staccato glimpses as the lightning would allow, she could make out a man, clawing through the mud towards them, three Hessians drawing up the hill after him.

"We have to retreat!" Lt. Davis hollered over the gale, fighting to turn the panicked horses.

"There's a man!" Mercy hollered back.

Lt. Davis squinted in the direction she pointed. "It's too late!"

The lightning flashed again, and Mercy looked hopelessly back at the man, who was now only thirty yards off with the Hessians closing fast. And she recognized him.

"Jonathan!" she gasped.

Without warning, she threw herself off the moving flatbed and into the mire. Scrambling to her feet, she raced towards him, her feet slopping through ankle–deep mud. She didn't know what she was going to do, only that she had to reach him first. She slid to a halt beside him, her lungs heaving, her dress hanging from her like lead. The Hessians, only a few yards away, their swords gleaming with every flash of lightning, hesitated, clearly surprised at her appearing.

All at once an idea hit her, and Mercy stuck out her arm and prayed. Through the driving rain, Theo came to land on her shoulder, shaking himself, before settling. The two of them glared menacingly at the Hessians. Mercy's hair and dress flapped wildly in the wind, her fists clenched as she stood between them.

Lightning flashed again, and she saw the Hessians pointing at her, their eyes wide with terror. Another flash and they began retreating down the hill looking over their shoulders to check her pursuit. Turning back to Jonathan, she jumped; Lt. Davis stood beside him, Jonathan's arm already around his neck for support.

"We need to go!" he shouted as the thunder cracked again.

Together, they loaded Jonathan onto the flatbed, and Mercy rode beside him as Lt. Davis drove the wagon. Everything was mud and rain, thunder and lightning, and darkness. Mercy trembled as the warmth of adrenaline was replaced by the chill of the storm.

Lt. Davis drove them as far from the battle as the horses would allow, but soon the road could no longer be determined for all the flooding. He pulled the brake; they were going to have to wait out the storm on the road. Using their bodies, the two of them did their best to protect their patient from the unrelenting gale.

After a couple of hours, the rains lessened, and Lt. Davis looked to Mercy, shivering. "We should try to find our army."

Mercy nodded back to him, her teeth chattering too violently to reply.

With a little encouragement, they were able to continue, though it was a struggle for the horses as much of the road was washed out or still under water. After a short distance, they came upon an officer and a small detachment of soldiers who had also weathered the storm out in the open.

"We've been ordered to regroup at Yellow Springs," the officer called out.

Lt. Davis saluted the man.

"It was the hand of God," the officer continued, wringing out his hat. "Mark my words. God Himself, rescued us this day. We were as doomed as ever we have been, and yet the Lord saw to it that we were hidden once more under the wing of His storm. God be praised."

"Amen," Lt. Davis agreed, slapping the reigns.

Mercy looked down at Jonathan, who'd fallen asleep. His sword wound was deep across his shoulder, but he'd recover. Wringing out her apron, she laid it over the wound, and climbed into the buckboard beside Lt. Davis.

"It was a miracle, wasn't it?" she asked.

"Aye, only the Good Lord could have gotten us out of that one," Lt. Davis said.

"I'm sorry for disobeying your orders," Mercy said, fiddling with her dress. "He's Adelaide's brother . . . I just couldn't leave him."

"Those Hessians thought you were a witch for sure," he sighed. "That was quick thinking, to prey upon their superstitions, but . . . I fear if you were ever to be captured . . ."

"I know, sir," Mercy said. "Folks burn witches."

"Rumors will spread amongst them; I'll make it my aim to see that day never comes. You're a better person . . . you make me want to be a better person." He smiled.

"We all must be better people if we're to make their sacrifices worth it," Mercy replied. "Otherwise, the new world will end up just like the old."

"Aye," Lt. Davis said, giving the reigns another snap.

When at last they arrived at Yellow Springs, Mercy was overjoyed to find Adelaide and Abigail already there busily attending to the wounded who'd arrived before them. The rain still fell softly and every minute more soggy soldiers arrived from where they'd been scattered, rounded up by cavalry scouts scouring the countryside.

"He'll be alright," Mercy said, holding her hand up in warning as Adelaide approached the wagon.

"Jonathan," she shrieked as she recognized her brother.

"He'll be alright," Mercy said again, wrapping an arm around her. "We need to get him dry, and the wound dressed proper."

Adelaide collected herself and nodded.

Together they brought him inside the meetinghouse–turned–temporary hospital and laid him on a table. Lt. Davis immediately went to work on him, not even stopping to dry himself.

"Mercy, go get changed, the wagon is behind the outbuilding. We can't have you catching cold," Abigail said. "Adelaide, why don't you go with her, it's going to be a bear to shrug out of that sopping dress."

Mercy obliged, and together they splashed their way to the wagon. Once inside, Adelaide fetched her other dress and together they got her changed.

"He really will be alright," Mercy said again.

"Did you see my Papa?" Adelaide asked.

"I could hardly see anyone," Mercy confessed.

"They always marched together," Adelaide said. "Papa wouldn't have left him out there alone." Adelaide's pleading eyes bored into her.

"I'm sorry, there were men retreating everywhere. A man could hardly have seen another man if they were standing right next to one another. Maybe when Jonathan wakes, he'll know better."

Adelaide nodded.

Chapter 20

September 20, 1777

 Today is a day both bitter and sweet. Word arrived from General Greene's regiment that Adelaide's papa was cut down by the Hessians near White Horse and is presumed dead. This news has come as a shock to all of us. It seems the heavy cost of freedom is ours to bear once again. To her credit, Adelaide has borne the news with dignity and finds reason to rejoice that she did not lose her brother as well. She asked that I help her pen a letter to her mama; it is a difficult request, but I could not refuse.

 Jonathan is healing well now that he is dry and warm. The wound was to the bone, and it will be a little while before we know if he'll have full use of his arm. As soon as the roads are passible, he'll be sent home to Boston to recover. Adelaide hasn't yet made up her mind if she will accompany him or stay, despite the fact she no longer has family here. The loss of a friend as dear as she, and even Mrs. Bell, creates in me a dreadful emptiness.

 The storm that proved our salvation has also severely depleted our munitions; our powder has turned to mud, and many muskets have rusted beyond use, though our scouts say the redcoats fared little better. The rain has finally stopped, but the debris of fallen trees and rutted roads makes travel near impossible. Things such as they are, we've all been given a moment of rest, except for General Wayne's regiment, who've been dispatched to keep an eye on the enemy.

We've received a bit of good news; British General Burgoyne advanced against General Gates near Saratoga at a place called Freeman's Farm, but the Americans were able to check his advance. General Gates is confident his position is strong, and his lines will continue to hold. For the first time in a month, the British advance has ground to a standstill. This news has greatly improved and revived confidence amongst the Continentals and, coupled with the storm, many believe providence is on our side.

Further good news, that funny Frenchman, the Marquis de Lafayette, who'd arrived in Philadelphia a short while back, was also wounded in the leg during the storm but has been sent to Philadelphia and will recover. Though he's a bit of a peacock, he's gained the respect of the army, and they rejoiced to hear he is doing well.

Once again, the cause has survived, albeit at great cost. In the morning, we will rise, raise our banner, and face the challenges that await us. The war is not over, and that is our victory.

Mercy Young, 14 years old

It'd only been a few hours since Mercy had laid down her diary and gone to sleep when shouting, followed by tromping feet, and the flicker of torch light cut her dreams short.

"What is it?" she heard Abigail ask.

"It's awful, ma'am," a man's voice trembled. "The doc sent me to fetch you. General Wayne's men . . . they've been butchered and burned in their beds! They're bringing the survivors now . . . by the wagonload. Ma'am, I ain't never seen anything like it."

"Good heavens!" Abigail gasped. "Tell the lieutenant we'll be right there."

"I'm up!" Mercy called as she began shrugging into her dress.

"I'm coming too," Adelaide said.

"Are you sure?" Abigail asked.

"I'm fine," Adelaide replied.

The three of them rushed across the soggy ground to the meeting hall. The man hadn't exaggerated, three flatbeds of moaning men were being littered into the hall, and Mercy could already make out their grotesque forms by torchlight.

Abigail covered her mouth with her hands as they entered the building. It was a sight beyond any they'd beheld, a room filled with suffering men, burned and slashed, in not but their night clothes.

Mercy stood frozen in horror in the doorway, until a gurney nudged her from behind, sweeping her to the side so another patient could be added. Lt. Davis moved rapidly from patient to patient, giving orders to those standing by to aid him.

Shaking herself from her daze, Mercy rallied her friend and they swept into the room, stepping over the bodies lining the floor.

Grabbing the arm of a young soldier standing by, Mercy ordered, "We're going to need water, all you can gather, and rags. Go now!"

The soldier nodded, shaking himself from his shock.

"Get some water boiling," Lt. Davis ordered. "We're going to need it. And more bandages! Any linen that can be spared, tear it into strips!"

"That's an order!" a well–dressed officer said.

Several more bystanders raced off into the darkness.

Mercy hovered over a patient; the man had been skewered twice with a bayonet in an arm and leg, and she set to work to control the bleeding.

"How did this happen, General?" Lt. Davis asked the well–dressed officer.

"We'd made camp for the night, I posted sentries, but they must have been taken by surprise. We'd been tailing the redcoats all day and the men were exhausted."

"Was it Indians?" Lt. Davis asked.

"No," the general replied. "These were regulars, somehow, they slipped round us. They come in quick and quiet, burning our tents as we slept, and slashing whoever fled. They had no mercy, they offered us no surrender. Some of my boys chose to burn in their tents rather than face the agony of the sword," his voice trembled.

"Who could order such a thing?" Lt. Davis whispered.

"It was the devil's work," the general said, dabbing one of his men on the forehead.

Mercy's heart felt heavy as she moved about the suffering; these boys had been massacred. Whiskey was given to as many as could stomach it, anything to dull the pain. This wasn't war, there was nothing honorable in this.

They worked through the night and all the following day. The final count from General Wayne's men: fifty-three killed, and more than a hundred wounded. Word was carried fast through the colonies, the brutal incident became known as the Paoli Massacre, named for where it had taken place. Rage filled the colonists at the dishonorable conduct of the British Army, and the ranks of the Continental Army swelled as rage gave new Patriots a cause worth fighting.

The attack, meant to spread fear, had the opposite effect. More colonists who'd been sitting on the fence, chose to support the cause. Badly needed supplies flowed in from the surrounding community and the Continental Army was refreshed and replenished. Not at all the spirit–breaking General Howe had had in mind.

Due to strategic necessity, Congress and General Washington elected to abandon Philadelphia and protect the army's supply line instead. They would move the capital to York, Pennsylvania. Though it was a blow to their pride, Philadelphia held no other strategic value. General Howe marched into Philadelphia on September 26th, assuming that by capturing the enemy's capital, he'd crushed the rebellion.

To his surprise, the Continentals did not surrender. A somewhat frustrated Howe divided his army, placing half in Philadelphia, and the rest in the strategic city of Germantown.

Though Howe had given orders against it, the redcoats looted Philadelphia, causing more frustration, even amongst the Loyalists, and souring their victory. While they seemed to be winning on the battlefield, they were losing in the hearts and minds of Americans.

Further frustrating British plans, General Burgoyne was still being held in check by Generals Gates and Arnold in the north. And the colonial cause was growing support by the day. Both scrappy American armies were still on their feet, and winter was bearing down on them.

The days following the loss of Philadelphia and Germantown were days of rest as the British occupied their newly conquered cities. Mercy, Adelaide, and Abigail worked in shifts caring for the victims of the massacre, while General Washington and his staff worked to find a way to respond to the British victories.

Adelaide had written her painful letter home, but decided to stay and continue to serve the cause until she received her mother's reply.

On a warm afternoon, Mercy and Adelaide walked slowly through the camp, taking a much-deserved break. The seasons had turned, bright red, yellow, and orange leaves adorned the trees, and the damp air was crisp. As they passed clumps of soldiers smoking pipes around crackling fires, the men would stop their chatter and nod to them politely, some of them shaking their heads in amused disbelief as Theo rode proudly on Mercy's shoulder.

"Thank you for staying," Mercy said as they walked.

Adelaide shook her head. "I know if I went home, I'd only fret and linger in sorrow. Here I'm needed, there's work to be done, and I have you and Abigail to keep my mind on better things. I hope Mama will understand."

"Me too," Mercy said, taking her hand. "You're the dearest friend I've ever had."

"And you're mine." Adelaide smiled.

"Once winter sets in, we'll have time for you to teach me more about knitting," Mercy said. "We haven't had time to touch our needles in months."

"I do miss it," Adelaide agreed. "It calms my anxious soul."

"You still writing to Ben?"

"Mmhmm," Adelaide replied. "Every night . . . I'm afraid he'll have a book to read when he returns. I tell myself I'm writing to him, but much of the time I'm just writing to myself. Getting out all the things I feel inside."

"Sounds like my diary," Mercy said. "When we get Papa back, I'm going to let him read it. That way he'll know that we didn't run and hide, that we kept up the cause in his stead. I want him to be proud of us."

"He will be." Adelaide smiled. "You're like no other girl I know, and I doubt any others know one like you either."

"You know, I've never asked you, what happened between you and Ben? I mean, one day we were all just kids and then . . . what changed?" Mercy asked.

Adelaide blushed. "I honestly don't know. We *were* just kids, but then one day I realized . . . I missed him when he wasn't there, it was like . . . an emptiness." She chuffed, "And I *really* liked it when he was there. Somehow an affection had grown while I was unaware. I didn't try to change . . . I just—did."

"Like . . . love?" Mercy asked.

"I don't know, how do you define it? I started watching, to see if I noticed a change in him. Little things, I'd think I saw something, only to doubt it later. But by and by, I noticed he began to take special care with me, he'd move to stand beside me, and I'd catch him staring at me." She glanced away to hide her smile. "In the moment I would always pretend I didn't notice, but later, I'd think about it and smile."

"Abigail says you're a smart match, but that your courtship should be long, and only wed after the war," Mercy said.

"My mama says the same. Who'd want to wed during a war? The strain on my heart is nearly too much to bear as it is," Adelaide said.

"You're good for him," Mercy said. "He's always behaved older, but you've managed to bring out the man in him."

Adelaide blushed. "This war has aged us all."

"That's a fact," Mercy agreed. "I look in the water pail, and I see my mama."

"She was pretty," Adelaide said.

It was Mercy's turn to blush.

Chapter 21

The mood in camp had shifted since the massacre and loss of Philadelphia. Though they'd suffered many losses this season, the Continentals seemed anxious for a fight. Cold early October mornings only fueled their fires; if they were to have a victory, it would need to be soon. Mercy could only imagine Howe's dismay that this testy little army refused to break.

Howe had beaten them in almost textbook fashion for over a month, taken their capital, and left them cold and damp out in the elements, and still they rose to fight. The pressure from England to finish the war was unrelenting, and the king seemed less interested in Howe's victories and rather faulted him for not finishing the job.

The ground was finally drying out; both commanders knew the fighting season was in its final weeks. Washington was spending long hours with his commanders each day scheming; another fight was surely on the horizon. Mercy knew better than to let herself get comfortable; the army would be moving out soon.

Stirring a fresh cauldron of bandages, Mercy tried to tune her ears to the gossip around her. She'd been at it a while, with little success, when Adelaide walked up.

"I got a letter from Mama," she said, adding more rags to the pot.

"And . . ." Mercy prompted.

"And she said it's good for me to stay." Adelaide beamed. "In fact, she said that once Jonathan recovers fully, she will return as well. She says this was my father's cause; it will remain our cause."

"She'd best wait until after winter. There's no need to suffer all that when there's no war going on. She'll have plenty to do in the spring," Mercy replied with a smile.

"You're right; I'll advise her to do so," Adelaide agreed.

"Abigail says we'll go home for Christmas this year, if it's the Lord's will," Mercy said. "It'll be nice to see the warm tavern again, along with Mr. and Mrs. Hadley. They say the boys have been right helpful; Abe shot his first deer just last week."

"It's as though they live in a dream," Adelaide said, closing her eyes. "How can they be only a two–day's ride from here?"

"It does strain the imagination, doesn't it?" Mercy agreed.

Together they lifted the bandages from the wash and hung them from a line to dry. As they were finishing, Abigail approached with one of her worried expressions on her face.

"Lt. Davis just gave me orders to start packing things up discreetly. It seems the army will be marching tonight. Most of the supply and medical teams will be dispatched to Whitemarsh, but a couple of flatbeds, the lieutenant, and Mercy, if you're willing, will leave with the army when it marches. He couldn't say where."

"I'll go," Mercy said.

"I wish you'd learn to say no," Abigail groaned. She closed her eyes as her shoulders sagged.

"I'll be okay, Mama," Mercy said, giving her an extra–long hug. "I always come back."

At dusk, with false fires burning bright, the army marched out once more into the night. Mercy noticed that each man had a square of white parchment in his hat, which seemed rather odd.

"Why do they have paper in their hats?" she whispered to Lt. Davis.

"It's so they can find one another in the dark, and determine friend from foe, should we encounter any before dawn. Much like a deer's tail."

Clever. "Are we marching to Philadelphia?" she asked again.

"Germantown. Two-thirds of Howe's men are garrisoned there. If we beat them in Germantown, we'll take back Philadelphia."

Mercy pulled her cloak tight around her shoulders; the humid air magnified the wind's chill. It felt like the battle of Trenton all over again. For the first time in over a month, the army moved out towards the enemy rather than retreat. They moved with anticipation and purpose, they moved with a vengeance.

Thick clouds limited the light of the moon, and coupled with dense fog, Mercy had trouble making out the ears of the horses pulling their wagon. She used to enjoy traveling, seeing so many towns she'd never visited before, but after the past month, she wished she could just stay in one place for a while. It was like being a pawn on a chessboard, constantly moving in hopes of gaining the upper hand.

A couple hours before dawn, the army splintered into four parts. Each part would move into position and hit Germantown in the wee hours of the morning, one from each direction: north, south, east, and west. If all went well, the redcoats would wake up to find themselves surrounded.

Mercy and Lt. Davis would wait at a safe distance on the northeast side of the town until their assistance was ordered. The night was spookily quiet except for a constant pitter patter of water droplets dripping on fallen leaves. The horses shifted in their traces, causing Mercy's heart to skip a beat. She willed them to be quiet for fear of being discovered by a British patrol.

Lt. Davis played nervously with the reigns beside her, tying and untying them over and over again, his foot bouncing continuously, causing the wagon to vibrate. Part of her felt for the British men about to be set upon, she'd been in their place, it was a most horrible way to wake.

As dawn approached, the tension mounted, like a string stretched to its limit about to snap. Mercy nearly jumped from the wagon as a cannon to her left rocked the silence, followed by another, and another. Below them, in the fog, Germantown was thrown into a frenzy. Patriot muskets fired as Continentals and militia reached the town and began fighting their way towards the British garrison.

In the beginning, the Americans clearly had the upper hand as the redcoats fell back into a stone mansion known as Cliveden, unable to withstand the American advance face to face. For several hours the battle ebbed and flowed in and out of the town. Neither side was able to gain an advantage.

Hoofbeats drew Mercy's attention from the battle as an officer approached them from the rear.

"We're going to need your services near Cliveden, Doctor," the man said. "We've taken heavy casualties from the house."

"Yes, sir," Lt. Davis replied, turning the wagon to follow after him. They rode a short distance before pulling up behind General Henry Knox's artillery. Several wounded Continentals lay in the dirt, while the guns continued to blast the mansion.

Hopping out of the wagon, Mercy grabbed the pail of water and a dipper and made for the nearest man. He'd been hit near the shoulder but seemed to be suffering the pain well. Ladling him some water, she looked as he sat up to see if the ball had passed through; it hadn't.

There were too many patients, and Lt. Davis couldn't get to them all before more were added. Carefully helping him lay back down, Mercy dug into Lt. Davis's bag. Finding the forceps, she placed a leather roll between his teeth. She'd never done this before, but she'd seen it done enough times to know what she needed to do.

"I'm sorry, sir, but I'm going to need you to be brave," she said. "If you wouldn't mind placing your hands under your backside . . . it'll help greatly if you don't try reaching for me."

The man nodded, sliding his hands under his bottom. When he was ready, he gave her an uneasy nod, his face already growing pale.

Mercy rinsed her tool, before holding it in trembling fingers above the oozing hole. After a silent prayer and a deep breath, she carefully guided the tips into the hole. The man tensed as she bumped into a hard object. As carefully as she could, she opened the jaws of the forceps as wide as the hole would allow, and then a bit wider.

Her patient went rigid as she pressed against the sides of the wound. Sliding the forceps in still further, she could feel the object grind against the ridges of the tool. When she felt she'd gone far enough, she bit down, pinching the musket ball. Holding firmly, she guided the forceps back out of the hole; breathing for the first time as the ball exited the wound.

Her patient panted heavily beside her, having himself held his breath.

Mercy turned, fighting off an impulse to vomit as emotions and relief washed over her. Taking the ladle, she poured fresh water on the wound.

"I'm going to need you to sit up if you're able," Mercy said. "So I can wrap you up proper."

The man nodded his sweat–soaked head, and with her help was able to sit up.

Mercy bandaged his arm, and helped him get to the flatbed, laying him beside one of Lt. Davis's patients. Turning back to the line of wounded, she thanked God for guiding her through that one, while praying over the next. The cannons fired again, filling the hazy atmosphere with more smoke, hiding her patients from her sight for a moment.

Adrenaline willed her forward, enabled her to focus on her task while the world blew itself to pieces all around her. Patient after patient, she worked until they had loaded them all and were off to Whitemarsh. The wagon was piled with wounded, yet the battle continued to rage as they pulled away. She knew there would be many more when they returned.

As the sounds of war faded, she felt herself begin to relax.

"You did excellent, Mercy," Lt. Davis said. "Soon your skills will rival my own, this army is blessed to have you."

Mercy wiped her bloodied hands on her apron. "I feel so helpless sometimes," Mercy said. "So desperate to save the ones I know I can't."

"That is our burden," Lt. Davis sighed. "To fight desperate, hopeless battles, because everyone deserves to know they are worth fighting for."

"I hear the grave diggers shovels even in my sleep," Mercy said, her emotions beginning to bubble up. "Reminding me of all the one's I wasn't enough to save."

"I'm so sorry, Mercy," Lt. Davis said. "It isn't right for you to know this pain."

"No," Mercy shook her head. "I fear the ungrateful person I'd be if I didn't know it. I wake up every day entirely grateful to be a part of this country, to be American, because I've seen with my own eyes, our spirit, and our sacrifice."

"You were only a girl when I met you," Lt. Davis said. "I can't even remember that girl now. You've grown up unfairly fast, Mercy Young. I pray that your sacrifice is justly rewarded."

"I think I've come to realize there's nothing fair in war, the expectation is unreasonable and foolish to hold. We can't choose what unfairness will come our way, only who we will be in spite of it. I may not be able to change the war, but I can continue to change myself."

"General Washington should have you write his speeches," Lt. Davis smiled.

"He has Martha for that," Mercy scoffed.

"Well, if I ever make general, you can write my speeches."

Chapter 22

In the end, the attack on Germantown had to be withdrawn, but not before the Americans had proved they were far from finished. Even as the army retreated to Whitemarsh, morale was high. They'd shocked General Howe for once, going toe to toe with the redcoats on their turf and inflicting heavy losses. The British general had been sure the Patriots would scatter after taking their capital, but now he knew they'd only be beaten when he took their spirit.

Further good news arrived on October 8th. General Gates, supported by General Arnold, defeated the British General Burgoyne in a major battle at Saratoga on the 7th. The British commander and chief and his entire northern army were completely surrounded and on the brink of destruction. The Patriots were winning.

Cheers went up all around camp as the news spread. General Burgoyne's army would not be joining General Howe; the rebels were holding—and defeating—the greatest empire in the world. Only a week earlier, they'd been on the brink of destruction themselves, but their spirit would not be broken, these Americans would only be satisfied with liberty or death.

Mercy found herself smiling with pride as she worked. She couldn't wait to hear Henry and Benjamin's stories when they returned. Her family, joined by so many others, was doing the impossible. The British may have captured Philadelphia, but the Americans were about to capture an army. Victory no longer seemed like a fantasy, but a growing reality.

But the war wasn't over . . . yet. Howe was already on the move, attacking Fort Mifflin on the Delaware River in an attempt to secure the waterway supply line to Philadelphia. General Washington knew that the longer the fort could hold, the harder things would get for the British hoping to spend the winter occupying Philadelphia in warmth, security, and entertainment.

For now, Mercy and the rest of the continental army were safe at Whitemarsh from where General Washington could monitor the British in Philadelphia and protect his supply lines. It was a much deserved, much needed respite. And as things quieted down, the girls could finally take the time to get away.

Frost–laden grass crackled under their feet as Mercy and Adelaide made their way down to the creek. That morning, Abigail had given them the day off, they'd collected Mercy's snares and Theo, and set out to have some fun. Taking their time, they picked their way along a deer path, enjoying the sun's warm rays.

Glistening water rolled painted leaves over smooth stones as they walked along the edge of the stream. The war had driven them to so many beautiful and wild places that nearly defied imagination. Places of healing and peace . . . if war didn't soil them.

"How are you doing?" Mercy asked as they stopped to set a snare in a briar patch.

"I'm alright," Adelaide said. "Though when things get slow, I ache for Papa."

"I hardly knew him. What was he like?" Mercy asked.

"Quiet, and sad sometimes. I think he often felt like he wasn't enough. Enough for Mama, enough for God, enough for himself. I think he thought that if he tried hard enough, everyone would be satisfied with him, and it wasn't that we weren't, but maybe we forgot to tell him that he was . . . enough."

"My papa was often the same: working himself to the bone, but always wishing he could've given more. I know he carried a terrible burden of hope for us, that we would know a better life than the one he'd known. That's what drew him out onto that green, his hope that we'd have a better life," Mercy said. "I think all good papas feel that weight."

"I hope he's at peace now, and that Mama can find peace too. It isn't going to be easy being a woman without a husband," Adelaide said.

"That's a fact," Mercy agreed.

"What about you?" Adelaide asked.

"I miss my papa too. I have no way of knowing if he's living or has passed. When this all began, we'd set out to fetch him back, but now, I don't know if I'll ever see him again."

"I feel that ache may be more difficult than mine," Adelaide said. "At least I know what's become of mine."

"It does confuse my heart," Mercy agreed. "Especially since Abigail and Henry took us in."

"That looks perfect," Adelaide said, admiring Mercy's snare.

"Thanks, we'd better set another over there just in case," Mercy said, pointing to another tunnel.

"Do you think we're the only girls to ever do this?" Adelaide asked.

"No," Mercy said. "Mr. Hadley said that native girls do all sorts of trapping and fishing, they skin the pelts of critters, build fires . . . sometimes with babies on their backs."

"Mama says they're savages."

"Mr. Hadley would disagree. He says they're different, but no better or worse. He told me they work hard, have a great respect for the land and creatures, they don't waste or destroy, but rather steward the land they live on. He told me that, in a lot of ways, they're a nobler people than we are."

"Have you ever met one?" Adelaide asked.

"No . . ." Mercy said, looking at the ground. "I saw a wounded one once, that day we were attacked on the road, and I—I just walked on by."

"I remember it. The army wouldn't have let you help if you'd wanted," Adelaide said.

"To this day, I still don't feel right about it."

"I've heard stories of terrible things done to folks," Adelaide said.

"Me too," Mercy said. "But I've seen people like us do terrible things to each other also. That last massacre wasn't Indians."

"I guess all peoples are capable of good things and bad things," Adelaide said.

"I reckon," Mercy agreed. "We should probably keep heading up this way, look for another thick patch or blowdown, there ought to be plenty, given the season we've had."

After hopping a small tributary, they came upon a large evergreen tree which had blown over in the storm, creating a labyrinth of thick branches. Here and there strips of bark had been chewed away by rabbits and other rodents who'd created perfect tunnels about the perimeter.

"There must be a dozen openings, we won't have enough snares to cover them all," Adelaide said.

"We'll have to do the best we can. If we disguise them well enough it will only be a matter of time before one chooses our snare," Mercy said, squatting down and uncoiling her remaining snares.

After dividing what was left, the girls went to work. It was sticky. Mercy snapped off twigs and branches that oozed thick, clear sticky sap that got all over their hands and aprons. Once applied, it was terrible tricky to get off.

Adelaide was becoming quite proficient at setting snares, only needing Mercy's help to hold the sapling when setting the trigger. It was a cumbersome undertaking for anyone and could lead one to desire to use words that were quite unladylike.

When they were finished, the snares were invisible, hidden by wispy pine needles. Theo, who'd fallen asleep during the process, woke as they admired their work, but seemed eager to continue their adventure rather than stare at some messy ol' tree.

The girls gave washing their hands one final go, before giving up and starting back to camp.

"This pine pitch is a regrettable substance," Adelaide complained. "Neither of us will be allowed to touch food or patients with hands like these."

"Abigail will know how to be rid of it," Mercy said confidently.

"It smells nice though," Adelaide admitted.

"Need to rub some on the boys when they get back," Mercy mused.

Adelaide burst out laughing. "Mercy Young, you are the most humorous person I've ever met."

When they arrived back at camp, Abigail indeed had a solution to their problem. She poured precious ale over their hands which miraculously caused the sap to release its hold and wash away. Mercy marveled at how a single woman could know so much.

That night Mercy went to bed thinking about rabbits in snares rather than war. She prayed for her family, thanked the Lord for their victories, that He'd carried them through their losses, and that in the coming days, they'd enjoy some rabbit stew.

Chapter 23

October 16, 1777

    Today was my birthday, and the rest we've been blessed to enjoy is a gift in itself. Mr. Hadley sent more snares, which arrived yesterday, though Abigail wouldn't allow me to open them until today. I wish the boys could have been here, Henry and Benjamin too. Life seems awful empty without my dearest folks in it.

    I'm fifteen now, nearly a grown woman, time seems to have passed so quickly. I feel torn between two worlds. Part of me longs to stay like a child; I enjoy the silliness and freedom from expectation that is a child's. But I also enjoy the responsibility and privileges of being an adult. I enjoy learning new things, rising to the challenges this life has brought to me, and being a part, rather than an observer, of the events shaping my world.

    Perhaps I still have time to be a little of both, or perhaps, like Mr. Hadley, I'll find a way to stay both. Even Mrs. Bell seemed to be learning that it wasn't necessary to sacrifice one in order to make room for the other, rather, the balance seems to be more about knowing when a little foolishness is alright. And those who have difficulty understanding when, are then called upon to abolish it entirely, or are considered fools themselves.

I'd never have guessed growing up would be so complicated. I find there are many expectations put upon me of which I am not even aware—until I fail to meet them, that is. Then, all there is left to do is apologize and learn and try not to get caught up in the disappointment of others. Abigail says I can't change what other people think, I can only change myself. I am always thankful for her patience.

Adelaide and I were excited to find two plump rabbits in our snares this morning, we would have had a third, but it appears a coywolf, or perhaps a fox, is on to us, leaving us only tufts of fur for our efforts. Even so, we had more than enough rabbit for a delicious stew on my birthday, and that'll put a smile on any girl's face.

I hope and pray that in the days to come, we can be a family again. That the Good Lord will continue to lead us down this difficult and right path though the days grow long, and our endurance is so often tested. I pray for renewed determination every day to see this contest through to the end with all the zeal due such a task. May we endeavor to earn our place in a better world.

Mercy Young, 15 years old

Within three days of turning fifteen, Mercy received one of her wishes. Cut off and surrounded, British General Burgoyne surrendered himself and the entire northern army to the Continentals on October 18th. Generals Gates and Arnold had done it. Henry and Benjamin would return to camp victorious.

At Whitemarsh, General Washington's army was elated with the news. Soldiers patted one another on the back as they listened and danced to fiddle music around warm fires. It was the Americans' biggest victory since Boston, and word was spreading that the French may even consider allying with America after such success.

Along with the shouts of triumph, came further murmurs of complaint against General Washington. Some said Gates was a more suitable commander and chief, seeing that he'd won a major victory and Washington had not. Many, it seemed, felt that winning the war via retreat was less noble than winning it through victories.

Lt. Davis argued that to a country with little money, retreat was the cheaper, and possibly, only way to win. To get the war on an even playing field, the Americans needed to deplete British resources to their level. And in his humble opinion, Washington was doing just that.

But, as is often the case, not everyone understands the big picture. To those folks, General Gates was a clear solution to the dismal results Washington had achieved thus far. When Gates returned, Washington would surely have another battle on his hands.

Mercy admired General Washington; the weight of the nation was on his shoulders, and after so many running battles, he'd still been able to keep the army together, and outsmart the British on numerous occasions. She'd ask Henry when he returned what he thought of General Gates after serving with him for a while. Perhaps they both made great commanders.

"I hear your father may be returning soon," Lt. Davis said as Mercy helped him bandage a patient who'd been wounded in a shootout with a British foraging party.

"Yes, his letter said to expect them any day now," Mercy said, after realizing he'd meant Henry.

"I'd love to be a fly on the wall when King George gets word of their victory. I'll bet he turns red as a strawberry," Lt. Davis said.

"I wonder what it's like for the people who live there, in England. Are they suffering because of the war, or do they go about their day as though there is no war at all?" Mercy asked.

"I'm sure their purses are feeling the pinch a little bit," Lt. Davis said. "Their army must be paid, whereas ours hasn't been paid in months."

"But they will be, won't they?" Mercy asked.

"I'm not sure," Lt. Davis said. "The truth is, from what I hear anyway, there isn't anything to pay them with. It's probably another fact about this war that is baffling the enemy."

"Mercy! Mercy!" Abigail cried, bursting into the tent. "They're coming! The riflemen are coming, the advance party for General Gates!"

Mercy looked over at Adelaide, and then to Lt. Davis expectantly.

"Run along, I'll finish this up," he said with a smile.

Mercy hung up her apron and raced after Abigail and Adelaide. Reaching the road, the camp was already in an uproar as the riflemen made their triumphal entry. Mercy found herself jumping up and down, trying to see over the heads of many a jubilant man and woman. The merriment was so overwhelming, she found herself smiling just because she was a part of it.

"I see them!" Abigail said, grabbing the girl's hands.

Abigail forced her way through the crowd, ploughing through soldiers and civilians alike, until the three of them were wrapped up in a combined hug by Henry and Benjamin. Involuntary tears rolled down Mercy's cheeks as her heart stopped holding its breath. They'd made it home, just as Henry had promised.

Henry kissed Abigail right there in front of everyone as Mercy squealed with delight, cupping her hands over her mouth. Benjamin gave Adelaide a long hug, perhaps their first by the look on Adelaide's face, but after a moment's hesitation, she hugged him back. Mercy took it all in, the sights and sounds, even the smells, she'd write it all down later.

She hadn't expected it, but it felt like having them back from the dead, and the relief of their return made a mess of her emotions. In the busyness of her work, she'd failed to realize just how much she needed them to be there.

Henry wrapped one of his arms around her and pulled her in tight, kissing her on the top of the head.

"I missed you every day," he said.

Mercy melted into him, allowing his presence to wash away the pain of his absence. She was finally safe again, safe and loved, she was home.

Abigail led them to their wagon. Henry got a fire going, while Mercy, Adelaide, and Benjamin went to check the snares. Abigail wanted to cook the men something befitting their return.

"Hopefully there won't be any skunks this time," Benjamin said as they walked along.

"We've been fortunate so far," Adelaide said, "although we lose a hare here or there to a coywolf or a fox."

"We had one of those critters stealing from us the year Mr. Hadley taught us," Ben said.

"Mercy told me," Adelaide replied. "But you were finally able to catch him."

"We did, Henry scared Abe nearly out of his skin while we were recovering it," Ben said.

"I'd nearly forgotten about that," Mercy snorted.

"I doubt Abe has," Ben laughed.

Reaching the downed pine, they were disappointed to find their snares still set just as they'd left them. Thanks to Mr. Hadley, they'd set a few more a little further down the trail. Arriving at a dense thicket, their efforts paid off, not with hares as they were expecting, but with two plump brown birds which hung lifeless from the wire.

"They look like chickens . . . only slightly smaller," Ben said. "It's been a while since I've seen one, but the name grouse comes to mind. I think Papa shot a couple near Lexington when we were younger. They're terrible hard to spot until they burst from their hiding place."

"I think I remember them too," Mercy said.

"If they're anything like chicken, they should be delicious," Adelaide beamed.

Ben carefully released them from the noose, and the girls reset their snares. The thicket was sure to be home to many critters.

On their way back, Adelaide and Ben walked arm in arm while Mercy brought up the rear. Ben seemed so much older now, he too was being transformed by the circumstances thrust upon him. He looked after Adelaide with all the respect and care their papa had looked after their mama, and Henry did for Abigail. Mercy made sure not to take her role as chaperone too seriously.

People loving people—that was something not even the war could take away. Mercy supposed that was because it was simply love's nature. Light shines without regard for the darkness around it because its nature is to shine. If light allowed darkness to hinder its shining, it would have to give up its very nature and cease being light. If that day ever came, how dark and lonely the world would become.

They were all heroes in this battle of light and dark. Not because they'd won every battle, but rather because in their many losses, they never surrendered the light and hope of freedom, they never gave up on each other. Their love confounded an enemy who only fought for those who'd sent them, while the Americans fought for those who depended on them.

"Blessings of the Lord!" Abigail exclaimed as they returned with the grouse. "I always felt it a danger to have you girls wandering the woods doing the sort of things a man ought to do, but in these times, we've eaten better than most thanks in large part to your adventurous ways. I suppose I'll have to thank Mr. Hadley the next time I see him," Abigail said.

"I'll get them cleaned up," Ben said.

"Oh, it's so good to have you men back," Abigail said, growing weepy.

Henry put his arm around her, pulling her to his side. He kissed the top of her head, and Abigail closed her eyes soaking up his love. Mercy's heart melted, she loved the way they cherished each other, and it made her feel warm all over.

Ben finished with the grouse, and since Abigail had already prepared a stew in expectation of rabbits, they had grouse stew instead. The warm broth felt heavenly as it ran down Mercy's throat. She'd learned to savor such moments, when everything was right, to carry her through the moments when nothing was.

As they ate, Henry and Benjamin shared their stories from the battles in Saratoga. How, on two separate occasions, General Arnold had ridden into battle when hope seemed lost and turned things around. His charisma and courage so inspired his men to push forward when their judgment had thought better of it, that they'd broken the resolve of Burgoyne's Indian allies, which left the redcoats cut off without scouts or supply. Then they laid siege to the British, who tried on many occasions to break free, but were repulsed by Arnold's quick action. During their final battle, General Arnold had been wounded in the leg, but he'd carried on in heroic fashion, refusing aid and rallying his men.

Though successful, General Arnold had been relieved of command for disobeying orders during the engagement and was awaiting court martial. Henry said not to worry, his men and officers would testify of his heroism on his behalf, and he'd be acquitted. No one who was present, could deny the role his leadership had played in their victory.

In the end, with no escape, and running desperately short on supplies, General Burgoyne had surrendered his army to General Gates. It was a blow that was sure to be felt all the way across the ocean in England. The British just might lose.

The fighting had been hard, and the sharpshooters had had a fair piece of it. Mercy could feel the weight each of them carried, the weight of hurting their fellow man, a terrible weight. They'd lost friends as well, men they'd come to know and respect, men who had families and dreams, but were no more. The history books would only tell of their victory, and the world would never know their great sorrow.

About the time they'd finished eating, Lt. Davis came by to fetch someone to help him with a procedure on one of the soldiers who'd come back from Saratoga. Mercy promptly volunteered, knowing Adelaide wouldn't want to leave Ben's side, and she could give Henry and Abigail some time alone.

When she arrived, Mercy donned her apron and met Lt. Davis beside the patient. He was young, maybe twenty, and she was all too familiar with his plight. His breech had burst, the rains over the past months had rusted the majority of Continental weapons, and those without the skills or proper supplies, were unable to repair the damage, leaving their muskets brittle and prone to burst.

It was obvious a field surgeon had removed most of the shards of metal, and the boy had been looking to the side when he fired, leaving his eyes intact. However, the bits which had been too small for the surgeon to find were now inflamed, and if not removed, could turn to gangrene.

"I'll need you to restrain him, while I remove the bits," Lt. Davis said.

"He's much too young and strong," Mercy said. "I won't be able to hold him. You restrain him, and I'll remove the bits."

Lt. Davis looked at her with concern. "Are you sure? It's an ugly business."

Mercy smiled softly. "I've seen plenty of ugly business before."

"Right," Lt. Davis sighed. "Have it your way, Miss Young. I will restrain him."

Mercy swung the lantern hook close to the boy's face. "I need you to be real brave," she said. "Close your eyes and focus on helping restrain yourself. We'll get the bits out quickly with your help, then, after you're cleaned up, you can rest."

Her words were soft, and the boy nodded his head, closing his eyes. Mercy picked up the knife and forceps and hovered over the first festering scab.

It took a little more than half an hour for Mercy to remove a dozen splinters of metal from the patient. To his credit, the boy never fought back, though his eyes ran with tears. The process was exhausting, and by the end, Mercy's hands trembled.

Lt. Davis cleaned the wounds with some form of alcohol and wrapped his face in a thin layer of bandages. After giving the boy a dose of ale, they left him to fall asleep.

Standing together outside the medical tent, Lt. Davis offered Mercy a warm cup of tea. "You did well, Mercy. As I've come to expect."

"Thank you," Mercy said, taking a sip. "You make a fine nurse," she teased.

Lt. Davis chuffed. "I'm glad your father has returned—I mean, Henry."

"It's alright, you can call him my father, my heart has already accepted him as such, and he's doing a fine job of it."

"Their victory has infused the army with a new spirit. I'm afraid all of Howe's work has been undone, our army will not be surrendering any time soon."

"And we'll be here, fighting for those who can no longer fight for themselves," Mercy said confidently.

"Aye," Lt. Davis said. "Oh, I got you something. I'd hoped to have them prepared for your birthday, but due to the rain, and our constant flight, some of them were soiled and needed to be redone."

Lt. Davis dashed into his quarters and reappeared with a stack of leather–bound journals. Hesitating for a moment, he placed them gently in her hands.

"They're my journals, of all my procedures and notes. Not to keep, but I know how much you like to read, and you absorb information like a sponge. I thought maybe you'd find them useful."

"I'd love to read them," Mercy gasped. "Thank you."

"I hoped you'd say that," Lt. Davis said. "There are a few personal anecdotes, you needn't waste your time on those."

"I'll take good care of them and have them back to you as soon as I'm through. You're rather courageous trusting your diary to someone else . . ."

"It's not that difficult, when you trust that person."

"Yeah, well the only one who's ever read mine is Abe, and I nearly skinned him alive," Mercy snorted.

"Abraham does seem to have his own way of doing things," Lt. Davis mused. "Though I suppose that is a trait shared by many a little brother."

Chapter 24

Following a month of minor skirmishes, on December 4th, a spy by the name of Lydia Darra sent word from Philadelphia that General Howe was leading his army out of the city in one final attempt to squash the rebellion before winter set in. Washington roused the army and set up a defensive position on the hills overlooking the Wissahickon Valley.

There, on the hills, the cause would make its stand. If they survived, they'd earn a few months' break while surviving the brutal New York winter. If not, Howe would go home a hero, and they would remain subjects of the king.

General Washington, as was his custom, had the Continentals build hundreds of fires in an attempt to fool Howe into believing the Americans were too strong, and call the whole thing off. Their supplies had already been moved to a safer location in order to prevent repeating the losses they'd encountered over the summer. Riders were sent out to keep an eye on Howe's movements; Washington did not want to be surprised again.

Henry and Benjamin's unit was always ready, they packed light so they could move quickly, and were often used to hold the flanking enemy in check until reinforcements arrived. It was a dangerous job. Mercy and the rest of the medical team waited behind the American artillery, far enough from the field to be safe, but close enough to observe.

At three o'clock the next morning, after a sleepless night, the alarm cannons sounded along the American line of defense; the redcoats were attacking. The new Continental recruits had quickly become well disciplined, and soldiers and militia raced to their positions preparing to meet the enemy.

Distant gunfire echoed ever nearer as the redcoats pushed back a colonial scouting party which was harassing them as they progressed. Mercy looked out over the valley in the direction of the conflict but the hills on the other side obscured her view. She shook with every cannon blast, her mind imagining its impact.

At last, the scouting militia retreated, folding itself back into the American lines; Howe was not far behind. By daybreak, British banners flew on the hilltops across the valley. Clouds of steam rose from thousands of anxious men as they waited for Howe to make his move, their commanders eyeing one another through the glass in a battle of wits.

Lt. Davis assured Mercy their defensive position was strong, and Howe must have believed so too because the moment his cannons were in place, he spent the remainder of the day shelling the American lines. Fortunately, their trenches were deep and strong, and Howe's guns on the hill were slightly out of range. The Americans were taking little damage.

If the British wanted to break them, they were going to have to face them.

Howe's cannons finally ceased at nightfall, and both armies prepared to endure the freezing cold night. No one slept well with the enemy knocking on their door. Mercy tried to keep her mind focused on good things, especially the part in the Bible that talked about the Lord preparing a table in the presence of their enemies.

Henry and Benjamin remained with their unit, and again Mercy felt her fragile world being ripped apart. She read Lt. Davis's journals by candlelight until her eyes burned with the effort. His notes were meticulous, endeavoring to expand his knowledge with every procedure. He faulted his ignorance for every loss, and she felt as though she was the only one who understood the weight of responsibility he bore.

And then she came to a familiar section, the night at Dorchester Heights. Finding her name amongst his words, she nearly closed the book as a wave of anxiety washed over her. Slowly turning back to the page, she read it. He'd praised her courage and endurance, saying she had exceeded all expectations any man could have laid on her. And he'd worried himself sick when she'd fainted of exhaustion.

Mercy blushed as she read. Did he really think so highly of her? She found herself itching to read more, while feeling a small amount of guilt for not passing over his personal thoughts. Somehow, she no longer felt tired; taking a deep breath, she turned the page.

In the morning, Howe marched directly at the American center and left flanks. Washington constantly shuffled his light units as needed, countering Howe's probing attacks. Mercy and the rest of Lt. Davis's team were kept amply distracted from the conflict by a steady stream of wounded militia and Continental soldiers.

Fortunately, Mercy was able to keep up with the goings on outside through the reports of her patients inside. The rebels were giving as good, if not better, than they were getting. A series of small strategic retreats repelled an attack by the Queen's Rangers and a Hessian light infantry unit, who tried to fold the American flank. A timely cavalry charge was enough to break up the attackers and put them in retreat.

So far, Howe was failing.

As the day progressed, several men from Henry's unit joined the ranks of those who'd fallen under Mercy's care. The British were fighting something fierce, but Howe was unable to make any useful headway. Mercy prayed for darkness, for the day to end and the concussive blasts to stop. She prayed for peace.

As new patients entered the tent, she found herself putting into practice the things she'd read from Lt. Davis's notes and decided she ought to begin her own medical journal. So much of their work depended on trial and error, and errors were costly.

She learned from a wounded rifleman that Henry and Benjamin, fighting in General Morgan's Rifle Corp, were slugging it out with General Lord Cornwallis on Edge Hill as the redcoats desperately attempted to turn the American flank. The hill had already changed hands several times that day, but the redcoats were beginning to push the riflemen back.

"We'll hold," Lt. Davis said, overhearing their conversation. "By God, we'll hold."

Mercy nodded her head and willed herself to focus on her patient.

Muskets and rifles cracked all along the valley outside. Cannons boomed, and orders were barked. Drums and bugles directed ranks of men through mud and smoke and violence as the king's wrath endeavored to stomp out freedom's spark.

And her work went on, cleaning wounds, applying bandages, holding hands, wiping brows. A few soft words to calm terrified boys. One last fight for the privilege to keep on fighting, and if not, a small taste of peace before the peace eternal.

She looked over at Adelaide, whose hair had come loose, bits of it escaping from a sweat–soaked bonnet that had failed to contain it. Streaks of blood adorned her rosy forehead where she'd wiped sweat with the back of her hand. She spoke softly, smiling warmly down at a boy not much older than Ben as she held his hand, dabbing his forehead with the other.

In a moment, she reached up and closed his eyes, laying his hand gently on his chest. Sensing Mercy, she looked up and shook her head. Mercy nodded, and aides standing by lifted the gurney and carried the boy away. There was no time now to mourn, to let it sink in; before the boy's body had even passed the veil of the tent, another was laid in his place, and Adelaide proceeded to tend to him. That was their work, hour after difficult hour.

At long last, the chill of night fell, and the fighting ceased as soldiers on both sides were forced to build fires to keep from freezing to death. While the combatants rested, Mercy, Adelaide, and Abigail continued working to save as many as they could, Lt. Davis moving from patient to patient as quickly as was prudent. None of them had taken the time to eat that day.

It was after midnight when the final patient was stable, and the four of them were able to get off their feet. Lt. Davis left to see if there was anything to eat, but he didn't sound hopeful.

Abigail sat down in the dirt and leaned back against a barrel. She closed her eyes, and in a moment was fast asleep. Taking a wool blanket, Mercy laid it over Abigail's shoulders.

"Tomorrow I'm working in my stockings," Adelaide said. "My feet are blistered, heel and sole, I can hardly move about."

"Mine too," Mercy groaned.

"How many did you lose today?" Adelaide asked.

"Four, maybe five," Mercy frowned. "You?"

"Four as well. They all remind me of Ben, and I have to swallow a panic that tries to overtake me."

"Here," Mercy said, dabbing away the blood on her friend's forehead.

"Thanks."

"Lt. Davis was right, we held them today, though I hear they took Edge Hill on this side of the valley. Morgan's riflemen had a long day today. Ben and Henry must be as exhausted as we are, hopefully they find themselves around a warm fire tonight," Mercy said.

Lt. Davis returned from his search for food empty–handed and exhausted. "All our supply has been sent away in case we're forced to retreat before daybreak. What little food there is has been distributed to the soldiers, I'm afraid I couldn't find us a crumb. You ladies must be famished after a day like today," he said mournfully.

"No more than you," Mercy said.

"Tomorrow is sure to be fiercer. The redcoats are running out of time before the winter and there is no doubt the king is demanding results since news has certainly arrived of their defeat at Saratoga. We must prepare ourselves body and soul for the day ahead. Collect dear Abigail, and get some rest, only Howe knows when the day will begin."

Chapter 25

The sun rose on the morning of the 7th to an eerie silence. General Howe had not marched out against the American defenders at first light, but waited, glassing across the smoke-filled valley of frost-covered mud and grass. Horses, harnessed to empty flatbed wagons outside the medical tent, pawed the ground nervously. Inside, the medical team laid out their tools, prepped bandages, distributed water pails.

"I wish the cocky bugger would just get on with it," Lt. Davis muttered under his breath.

Mercy and Adelaide bandaged each other's feet, too big now to fit into their shoes if they'd wanted them to. Lt. Davis looked over his team of exhausted nurses with sorrowful eyes.

"I'm dreadfully sorry for your poor care," he said. "I'm afraid there's nothing but my own shortcomings to blame for your neglect . . ."

"That's not true!" Abigail snapped. "This pitiful war has nothing to do with your shortcomings. We're all here because we chose to be, same as you. The Bible is filled with stories of those who went without the comforts of food and rest, and they rose up to follow their calling just the same. Were they not written to bring us strength to endure times like these?"

"Yes, ma'am," Lt. Davis said, nodding in agreement. "Thank you."

At noon British drums set everyone's hair on end; Howe was finally on the move. Immediately reports rode in of redcoats forming up for attack against their center and left flank once more. American cannons were loaded, cavalry mounted, orders dispatched.

Mercy held her breath, awaiting the fateful first shot.

And there it was, the distant thundering of Howe's cannons breaking the stillness, probing the American center. Outside the tent, American artillery opened up, shaking the ground under Mercy's feet, and momentarily deafening her ears. Everyone in the medical tent froze, helplessly awaiting the first victims of the day.

Mercy's empty stomach turned as the caustic sulfur smell of cannon smoke wafted into the tent, adding to the already nauseating atmosphere. Closing her eyes, she swallowed down the lump in her throat, as the first muskets of the day released a volley. The battle was on.

Mercy sent up a prayer for General Washington and his fellow generals, freedom's fate rested in their hands. She prayed for Benjamin, Henry, and the other men and boys desperately trying to hold on. And she prayed for General Howe, that he'd see the madness of the king's orders and withdraw his army.

As she finished, the first flatbed pulled up, four wounded men were rushed into the tent, and her work began.

"There—there's too many of them," the man on her gurney stammered. "They're marching right through us."

Mercy undid the man's breeches and slid them down revealing a deep bayonet wound to his thigh. To her relief, the wound oozed rather than spurted, which meant his artery was still intact. Rinsing the wound with water, she wiped away the blood just long enough to pour a bit of ale on it. The man went rigid with the pain.

"You'll be alright," Mercy said, confidently. "We'll have to change your bandages every day, but it'll heal if we can keep it clean." Gingerly she began wrapping the man's leg in fresh bandages.

"How is he?" Lt. Davis asked, sliding in beside her.

"He's fine, go on to the next!" Mercy directed. Before she'd finished talking, he was already gone. "Here," Mercy said, tipping the flask of ale on the man's lips. "It helps a little."

The man nodded, taking a sip.

"They're going to move you now, but don't worry, I'll check on you again."

A couple of boys not much older than Abe carried the man to the far side of the tent, just as another wagon pulled up outside. More men were unloaded, and Mercy moved on to her next patient.

This man was far less fortunate than the first. Two musket balls had struck his lower abdomen; he was clearly in great pain. Again Lt. Davis slid in beside her.

"Give him some ale, and set him outside," he ordered the two aides who were standing nearby.

As they lifted the gurney, Mercy reached for it, holding it back.

"Mercy," Lt. Davis said, firmly grabbing her hand by the wrist. "There are too many today, you have to let him go."

Reluctantly Mercy let the gurney slip from her fingers, and watched as it was carried through the back flap of the tent, where the man would be left to pass alone. Exhaustion and pain welled up inside her and her eyes overflowed, allowing heavy tears to roll down her cheeks.

"I'm sorry, Mercy," Lt. Davis said, releasing her hand. "We have to concentrate on the ones we can save."

And another patient was laid in front of her.

"Scissors, please, Mercy," Lt. Davis asked, pulling her from her pain.

Mercy handed him the scissors and together they began treating a lower leg wound. She knew it was the same for Abigail and Adelaide, and even Lt. Davis, though he was better able to bury his emotions. It was apparent by the heavy commotion of battle outside that Howe intended to break them today.

Hour after hour Mercy worked as patents rolled in at an impossible rate. Yet, hour after hour, the flag of liberty flapped unincumbered just outside. The king's army raged with incredible fury, as waves of British regulars smashed up against American defenses that bent but would not break. The resolve of Liberty baffling its invincible foe.

Mercy wore through her stockings, determined to match the resolve of those she treated. Her dress was wet with sweat, her head pounded relentlessly, her muscles ached from head to toe, her eyes burned with tears she wouldn't let fall. Through grit teeth she washed, bandaged, splinted, applied ointment, lifted, carried, ladled . . .

Then came the silence. How long it was before she noticed it, she couldn't be sure, but there it was. Looking about her, she realized the sun had long since set, the tent was only dimly lit now by the light of oil lanterns hanging from iron hooks.

She looked towards the flap, but no new patients were carried in. Around her, Abigail, Adelaide, and Lt. Davis continued to work as though nothing had changed. Finishing tying the bandage she was working on, Mercy limped to the flap and opened it. Her knees went weak as she drew in the first breath of cool fresh air.

Below and across from her, the valley was aglow with hundreds of fires as exhausted soldiers warmed their exhausted bodies, having survived another day. To her surprise, she saw four horses riding towards her, one was a white horse, and the rider was familiar. Reaching the tent, General Washington dismounted and made his way towards her.

"It's Mercy, isn't it?" he said, removing his hat.

"Yes, sir," Mercy said with a curtsy.

He frowned at her. "Are you alright?"

Mercy nodded.

"My I?" he asked, gesturing to the tent.

"Of course," Mercy replied, holding the flap open.

General Washington stepped inside, and Mercy followed him. Abigail nearly fainted when she turned to see him.

"How are we?" General Washington asked.

"My staff is tired, sir, but resilient," Lt. Davis began. "Though we haven't eaten in more than a day."

Again, General Washington frowned. "I'll have one of my aides send over whatever can be found. For your services, I cannot thank you enough. No one knows the tally of freedom's cost more than you. I believe General Howe thought to make an end of us this day, yet our banner still flies."

"How much longer can we endure?" Lt. Davis asked, wiping bloodied hands on a bloodied rag.

General Washington hesitated, looking long at the doctor, before his face softened. "If it were to be another day such as today, I don't know. Lord knows we are exhausted, short on supplies and munitions, and soldiers. Yet, that seems to be often the case, and our boys rise to the occasion again and again. For three days we've endured the king's might, that's three days longer than anyone would have thought possible when we began. I believe there is victory yet to be had, so long as we continue to believe in it."

"Yes, sir." Lt. Davis responded.

"I'll send my aide with food as soon as possible;` make sure your staff gets some rest,"

"Sir."

After speaking with a few of the wounded, General Washington ducked out of the tent and rode away. Many of the wounded had been transported further away to military hospitals to recover. Most of those who'd been left behind had minor wounds and would return to the army in a week's time. If the cause survived that long.

Keeping his word, Washington's aide appeared a short while later with a barrel of apples and blocks of cheese. It was an odd combination, but as Mercy bit into the first apple, she felt as though she were in heaven. The juice seemed to wash away the day as she finished the first and moved on to the second. Adelaide, who was ever proper, bit into her apple with ravenous hunger, not waiting to finish the first bite before taking another.

As the food filled them, hope seemed to follow, and Mercy felt life returning to her exhausted limbs. Now all she needed was a warm bath, but she'd settle for being full.

"Come along, girls," Abigail said. "You'd best get me back to the wagon before sleep takes me right here and now."

Mercy nodded, and together the three of them limped and staggered back to the wagon.

The following morning, Mercy was shocked to find the canvas glowing with warm sunlight by the time she woke. Slipping painfully from her blankets, she donned her dress over exhausted muscles, and climbed gingerly down from the wagon. Abigail and Adelaide met her just outside, sipping tea by the fire.

"What's going on?" Mercy asked. "It's nearly ten."

"I was startled myself, when I woke," Abigail began. "But I managed to find the doctor and he told me that the British broke camp early this morning and are on the road back to Philadelphia." She smiled, taking Mercy's hand. "Our boys held 'em, Mercy."

Mercy nearly fell over; it had seemed so desperate as she'd fallen asleep, and now, they'd won? "You're sure?" Mercy asked.

"Lt. Davis said they'd send out scouting parties to make sure Howe isn't up to his old tricks, but yes, it seems they've given up the fight," Abigail said, eyes brimming with tears.

Mercy stepped forward, giving her a hug. In their embrace, her muscles relaxed as another weight of fear she'd grown accustomed to carrying, melted away.

Cheers rose up form trenches and hilltops as the news spread of the British departure. The scrappy Continental Army kept defying everyone's expectations, even their own. Just over her shoulder, at the top of the ridge, the Star–Spangled Banner waved proudly in the frosty air. The spirit of freedom herself, rejoicing with them that so many a common person would not abandon her cause.

Mercy met Lt. Davis at the medical tent, who bowed respectfully with an invigorated snap. "Good morning, dear Mercy," he said.

"Good morning, sir."

"I trust you've heard the news?"

"Yes, sir."

"It looks as though we'll finally be rewarded with rest."

"Everyone deserves it, sir," Mercy agreed.

"Aye, and then we'll turn and face our other foe," Lt. Davis said.

Mercy scrunched her face in confusion.

"Winter," he sighed.

"Mama always says there's no rest for the weary."

"And we be they," Lt. Davis agreed. "Though I find winter a more predictable adversary."

"Once the army has settled in a winter camp, Abigail says we're going to return to the tavern for a couple weeks to be with the boys and Mr. Hadley."

"You will be missed," Lt. Davis said. "But it is well deserved."

"I'm sure you could join us if you were inclined?"

Lt. Davis looked through the flap in the tent. "It's true I have no family to visit, but my work is enough. Who would tend to the boys if I were to go with you?"

"You have other aides, most of the wounded have been sent away . . . it'd just be the frost and fever, and those awful scabies they'd have to contend with."

"I appreciate your kindness, perhaps I'll join you next time," he said. "For now, I think rest is what I need, and I will likely find more of that here."

Mercy nodded. "Just make sure you take a little time for joy come Christmas. It isn't good to be so utterly serious all the time."

"Utterly serious?!" Lt. Davis balked. "I have plenty of merriment."

Mercy stared at him blankly.

"Well, perhaps I could learn to be merry again," he scoffed.

"Mrs. Bell always says a person can learn anything as long as they're willing."

"I am," he smiled.

"That's a good start."

Chapter 26

December 25, 1777

Tonight, I lay warm in a goose down bed piled high with warm blankets. My stomach aches from being full of ham and potatoes, and of course sugar plumbs. The tavern is filled with the smells of spices and pipe smoke, and the hushed tones of Henry, Mr. Hadley, and Ben as they talk of the war and the coming year. My heart doesn't know how I ever allowed myself to be torn from this place.

This afternoon, the reverend held service and recounted the birth of our Savior. Such a humble beginning for a king, though His empire is an empire of love, not like the empire of King George. Afterwards, in the example of the magi, we exchanged gifts with one another. Mostly small things as there is little money amongst us.

Mr. Hadley gave me a beautiful skinning knife with a handle made from a deer's antler. Abigail scoffed, she doesn't believe ladies should receive such gifts, but Mr. Hadley said a good sharp knife is a handsome gift for anyone, lady or not, and I agree. Even Theo was given a fresh mouse which had gotten caught lurking in the pantry.

In the absence of my own mama and papa, the Lord has given me a family beyond any I've ever known. Where I once felt empty and alone, I now feel full and loved. We fit together in a way that could only be defined as miraculous; and I find myself overcome with joy as I watch David bounce on Henry's knees, or Mr. Hadley wrestle Abe while Mrs. Hadley and Abigail shriek in protest. It is a sight most wonderful.

Adelaide went home to visit her family in Boston, she will return to the camp with the Bells and our boys in the spring. We've only been apart a week and already I miss her terribly. I write to her daily, and the post rider is always kind enough to come for my letters when he's around.

I also find myself missing Lt. Davis. I wrote to him so that he'd receive a bit of joy this season. He's become family too . . . after a sort, and I worry he'll not take a break if I'm not there to direct him. I know he pushes himself so out of desperation to prove to his father and himself that he is a worthy man. I wish they could manage to forgive one another; family is not something to cast away so lightly. Sometimes in the hotness of our tempers, we become blind to what it is we're burning.

After the new year, we will once again board our wagon and return to camp at Valley Forge. The army has constructed small cabins to help overcome the cold, though the snow has been exceptionally deep, making even simple tasks a great effort. Meanwhile, the British are warm and well entertained in Philadelphia. It infuriates me to no end, like having a fox

wintering in the hen house. Henry tells me not to let them get under my skin,
but I don't see how that's possible.

Everything considered, I'm grateful for another year; for the blessings and
hardships, and the people who have endured it with me. No one knows what
the following year will bring, and I've learned it's better not to look beyond
tomorrow, today is enough. In the morning, we'll wake up, and face the
challenges that await us, together.

Mercy Young, 15 years old

With the new year, Mercy found herself being bounced around in the back of their wagon as the team struggled to pull it down snow–covered roads. Already she missed the warmth of the tavern, and her stomach churned with anxiety at the winter trials ahead. Still, Lt. Davis and the cause needed their help, and the Lord always made a way to get them through.

It made her smile to see Abigail nestled between Henry and Benjamin in the seat, resting her head on Henry's shoulder, soaking up every moment. Love was a beautiful thing. It made her feel safe and warm, the love they had for each other. After all the storms they'd endured, it'd only grown stronger.

When at last they reached the camp, they were greeted by Lt. Davis who seemed elated at their arrival. Although he'd suggested she wait until morning, Mercy donned an apron and went to work. The trip had stiffened her joints, and a bit of nursing was just what they needed to loosen up again.

It was no surprise with the bitter temperatures, that the fever had returned. Several of the patients trembled under their blankets as sweat poured from their faces. Lt. Davis informed her that their losses to the fever were a growing concern to the army as they were on pace to rival their losses in combat over the past year.

In the same way the battles tested their speed, the fever tested their endurance. The work was grueling, monotonous, and messy, and the outcome most often grim. Lt. Davis petitioned commanders to give their soldiers proper clothing and food but was always informed there wasn't any to give. If only there was someone willing to supply them.

Mercy came to hate the winter as much as she did the redcoats, there was an unrighteousness to a courageous man dying trembling in his bed. She prayed earnestly for the Lord's provision of what was necessary to sustain them through this most difficult season. Abigail too, wept often as a patient would die so needlessly under her care. It was difficult not to feel abandoned in the hopelessness of their plight.

But it wasn't all bad. Winter also meant rest for soldiers who'd toiled over so many months, and rest meant music around warm fires, laughter, and hope. Soldiers drilled in the field, became more proficient, more disciplined. New soldiers joined the cause, replacing those they'd lost, and the generals talked and argued over the spring campaign.

While she was working one morning, she noticed Lt. Davis acting rather odd. He wore his military coat, which he only wore in ceremony, and from time to time, when he caught her looking his way, he'd straighten it while standing at attention.

At first, she'd thought he was simply extra cold, and the added jacket provided some warmth, but as time went on, she found herself feeling rather awkward because of it.

"Is there something the matter?" she asked hesitantly.

"No, why?" he asked.

"Well, if you don't mind me saying, you're acting rather odd."

"Am I?"

Mercy nodded. "Did I do something wrong?"

"No—no, you haven't."

"Is there someone important coming to visit?"

"No. Why do you ask?"

"You're wearing your uniform. You usually only do that in ceremony, so it doesn't get messy while you work."

"Oh, yes, my uniform . . ." he stammered. "Notice anything different?"

Mercy studied his jacket for a moment. "Is there something different about your collar?"

"Ah, so good of you to notice." He smiled sheepishly. "I've been promoted to captain."

Mercy blushed. *So, that's why he's been acting like a peacock.* "You look very . . . commanding," she said.

"Thank you," he said, snapping to attention once more.

"You'd best take it off before it gets soiled, you wouldn't look quite so handsome then."

"You're quite right," he said. "Would you mind giving me a hand?"

Sliding the jacket off his shoulders, she folded it over her arm and handed it to him as he turned.

"You've more than earned it, sir."

He bowed, before taking the jacket into his quarters.

"I wanted you to know I finished your journals. I'll return them to you once our wagon is unpacked," Mercy said. "They've inspired me to start my own."

"Glad they could be of service," he said, emerging from his room. "I hope to publish my notes someday in a medical journal, that way future doctors can learn from what we've learned, and perhaps not so many would have died in vain."

"I think that's a wonderful idea," Mercy said.

A patient's persistent coughing drew them back to work, and as she walked to the man, she found herself grinning at Capt. Davis's silly behavior. He really *had* been strutting for almost an hour, and had she known why, she would have prolonged his agony for as long as he could endure. She nearly kicked herself for missing such a perfect opportunity.

It was half past ten when Abigail showed up to fetch Mercy and take her place. Though her feet ached, and she knew the night would be uncomfortably cold, Mercy was glad to be back. This is where she belonged, where she was needed, and her mind could be kept busy with her work.

As she went to sleep that night, with the wind and snow howling outside, she thanked the Lord for the storms. The storms that had hidden them during the summer campaign, and the storm that hid them now. The British would not leave the warmth of Philadelphia to march against them during a winter such as this. They'd rest securely, in the shelter of the storm.

Chapter 27

February 8th, 1778

After a long and harsh winter, General Washington shared news the likes of which I thought I would never hear. On February 6th, King Louis of France joined us in our fight for freedom. Soon, aid of every kind will be at our disposal, along with the strength of the French Navy and soldiers. Henry says this is grave news for the redcoats who will now be matched on land and sea.

This news could not have come at a better time, as our supplies are bitterly low, and desertions have become commonplace. The Cause itself was on the brink of self–destruction, but now, there is talk of taking the fight to the enemy and driving the redcoats from New England.

The anticipation of the coming season is powerfully optimistic, and I feel as though the army is like a bear rising from its den; anxious to shake off the winter and reclaim its dominion. The news of the alliance has awakened a hunger, a fire, to meet the enemy on even ground, and show them the depths of our determination.

Capt. Davis, in his usual stoic way, says that our work will be the same either way. Though I know he's right, I feel there's nothing harmful about a little hopeful anticipation. Abigail says that if I can soften Mrs. Bell, Capt. Davis should be easy. I deeply appreciate her confidence.

In a month's time, Mrs. Bell will return, bringing Abraham and David with them. Jonathan has recovered fully and has reenlisted with Mrs. Bell's blessing. They are a firm family and intend to see the fight through. I am anxiously counting down the days until we'll all be together again, and Benjamin is even more anxious than I.

Theo has been often gone as of late, and I feared he would leave me altogether, when just last night he returned to our wagon hooting loudly, and then another owl joined him. I believe there may be a Mrs. Theo, and I cannot fault my dear friend for following his heart. Soon he may have his own family, and I don't know what that will mean for us. Abigail says the Good Lord will sort it all out, but He doesn't always sort it out the way I'd like.

The coming year promises to be one of change. I pray that when I write a year from now, my family and friends are all safe and sound, and the enemy of our dreams is vanquished from this land. May God keep us, and my papa, in His care.

Mercy Young, 15 years old

Glossary
of Uncommon or Difficult Words

Adversary: A person or group who is fighting against you

Anecdotes: A short, interesting or funny story

Apt: Especially qualified for something

Astonishment: Extreme surprise

Bout: An outbreak or attack

Ceding: To yield or transfer ownership of something to someone else

Charisma: A magnetic charm that draws loyalty or admiration to someone

Comprehend: Understand fully

Condemnation: Blame

Contumely: Harsh treatment coming through contempt

Daft: Foolish

Depot: A storage facility for military supplies

Derision: To mock or make fun of, put to shame

Dispatches: Written messages to be carried to someone else

Forage: To search for naturally growing food

Foray: An adventure with the purpose of finding plunder.

Frigate: A swift, multi-sailed ship, heavily armed with cannons intended for war

Glass: To scan through a telescope

Glutton: To consume passionately (typically food) beyond what is reasonable.

Haphazardly: Without care or order

Hazardous: Very dangerous

Infirmary: A hospital or place to care for the wounded

Jubilant: Rejoicing, often triumphantly. To be exceedingly happy.

Meandered: Wandered slowly, without any planned direction

Meticulous: Extremely careful and precise

Monochromatic: Having only one color

Morality: The value of knowing right and wrong

Patrons: A paying guest

Percolating: Something (typically a liquid) seeping through a porous substance.

Prudent: To act with wisdom, to do what is wise after careful consideration

Quartermaster: Person in charge of supplies

Rash: To act without considering the consequences

Reconnaissance: To survey a situation or landscape before taking action

Resigned: To commit, even if it goes against one's wishes or better judgment

Resolution: A formal commitment or opinion

Romanticized: To embellish or imagine things in a romantic or more heroic fashion than they actually are

Scoured: Search thoroughly

Staccato: Disrupted or disjointed phrases

Vantagepoint: Typically a high place from which it is easier to view the landscape

Vigorous: To do something with a lot of energy, or a person who is full of life and energy

Zeal: Passion that burns like a fire inside

It's not over yet!

I'd love to help other readers enjoy this book as much as you have. If you'd just take a minute and let them know your favorite scene, how the story impacted you, or what book or author you'd compare it to, it will help other readers find it. It's your best way to show your support for us and we greatly appreciate it! Just scan this QR code to get to the Amazon review page and leave your review!

(Even if you purchased or received this copy from somewhere else, you're still eligible to leave a review on Amazon if you have an active account.)

Get your FREE Gifts from J. E. Ribbey!

FREE Story Quiz for Under the Wing of the Storm
with a separate answer key!

FREE Printable Map
including the battles of Oriskany and Saratoga

Scan Me

To get these FREE resources and to find out what happens next to Mercy and her family, scan the QR code or visit our website at JERibbey.com!

About the Author

J.E. Ribbey, a husband & wife team, deploys a compelling writing style, combining a fast-paced action thriller with deep character immersion, giving readers an edge-of-your-seat adventure they will feel in the morning. A combat veteran, outdoorsman, and survival enthusiast, Joel enjoys mingling his unique experiences and expertise with his passion for homesteading and the self-sufficient lifestyle in his writing. A homeschooling mom, homesteader, and digital designer, Esther brings the technical, editorial, and design skills to the author team. Together with their four kids they manage a small farmstead in Minnesota, where, besides taking care of the animals and gardens, they also run an event venue and small campground. If you'd like to know more, you can find the Ribbeys on Instagram @j.e.ribbey or at their website JERibbey.com.

Made in the USA
Thornton, CO
01/24/25 08:45:35

0367e8c7-b940-4455-aab2-bff25060753bR01